THE BOSS IN THE WALL A TREATISE ON THE HOUSE DEVIL

A Short Novel by
Avram Davidson and Grania Davis

COPYRIGHT

DEDICATION

To our beloved friends—
you know who you are.

INTRODUCTION

Welcome to Or All the Seas with Oysters Publishing, where you are about to embark upon a voyage into The Avram Davidson Universe. Within this Universe, you will find the works of Hugo, Edgar, and World Fantasy Award-winning and genre-transcending Avram Davidson, who is considered one of the finest authors of the 20th century, and the works of Grania Davis, Avram's onetime life partner and frequent writing collaborator, a dedicated preservationist of Avram's works, and a talented and acclaimed author in her own right. Or All the Seas with Oysters Publishing is dedicated to bringing both the out-of-print and the never-before published writings of both Avram and Grania back to life in print, audio, and e-book formats, and we look forward to making this treasured legacy accessible once again to readers, ranging from longtime fans and scholars to those just beginning this journey.

Avram's Universe is calling—we invite you to step inside.
avramdavidson.com/join-the-fan-club/

AVRAM

By Peter S. Beagle

And here I bloody go again, writing another foreword —my third—for one of that man's books. Other people wangle themselves profitable concessions, like Carlos Castaneda with his Don Juan, or all those people channeling 35,000-year-old Atlantean warriors who give stock-market tips. Me, if I ever channel anybody, sure as hell it'll be *him* calling from *Le Grand Peut-être*, asking me to find him a book even God and PosthumousNet can't locate. It's a bit like the time a lovely African-American actress named Tamu cornered me on the set of a TV movie I'd written, telling me with great delight, "This makes the second time I've played James Earl Jones' daughter. One more time, and I get to keep him!" Well, nobody would make a dime channeling Avram Davidson, but there would be compensations. You could definitely say that.

The Lascaux cave paintings were still a bit sticky to the touch when I first saw him across a crowded room at a Berkeley party. To be accurate, I heard him before I saw him: a short, wide, highly bearded man, looking like a cross between a Hasidic *rebbe* and W.C. Fields. He was explaining to a bewildered young person who had offered him a ride home that he'd backstroke from the Berkeley Marina to Molokai before he'd ever set foot in a Volkswagen, or anything else German. I'm easily impressed by principles, having so few myself. Besides, I knew who he was, and I'd been reading his stories—"The Golem," "The Certificate," "Help! I am Morris Goldpepper," "Ogre," "Now Let Us Sleep," "The Sources Of The

Nile," "Or All the Seas With Oysters"—since I was fourteen years old. I wanted to speak to him, but I was too shy then. He was Avram Davidson, and he walked home that night.

Or so I remember. Avram always insisted that the entire evening, Volkswagen and all, was a figment of my overheated imagination, and quite possibly Berkeley itself was too. He felt it would explain a great deal. Well, they were his poor, flat, gouty feet, and he certainly should have known how they spent their nights, so I'm sure he must have been right. Yet, true or not, that's really how I see him when I think of him now: gravely charming, intimidatingly gifted, by far and far the most learned man I ever knew; uniquely funny as a standup standoff between Lewis Carroll and S.J. Perelman, and perfectly capable of driving those who most admired and cared for him right up the damn wall. He was an easy man to care about—to revere, even—but hardly to live with. He knew it, too.

All right, I challenged him more than once, if that wasn't how we met, then how did it happen? Avram always shrugged. Who knew? and what did it matter? Here we were. For a man haunted and inhabited by history, he always seemed to live very much in the present moment. It's just that Avram's wasn't anyone else's present moment.

He knew everything in the world. My idea of a well-spent evening for twenty years was to set him up comfortably with a drink and a good meal and ask, "Avram, tell me Stuff." All I ever needed to know about Prester John, Aleister Crowley, "Rajah" Brooke, medieval cuisine, Chinese alchemy, Cornish folklore, mermaids, mandrakes and gloriously endless other Stuff, I learned from That Man. Not to mention the Stuff I learned while I was learning, for Avram was a master of the irresistible digression, the dangerously alluring detour. He was, for me, a combination of Odysseus, Tiresias, Samuel Johnson, Pliny the Elder and the British Museum.

We wrote to each other a lot (it'll be easy to publish the Collected Letters when the time comes, because I can't imagine anyone not keeping a letter of Avram's), and our salutations grew more and more elaborate as the years of correspondence passed. Mine ranged from a simple, manly "All-Highest, sir," to "O great Piebald Elephant of Wisdom and Good Personal Hygiene," while Avram's might well read, "Estimated Dom Pedro, Viceroy of the Western Hesperides, Absentee Landlord of Huy Braseal, Hereditary Head *Mohel* to the House of Saxe-Coburg." I was invariably Dom Pedro to him. The letters always ended, on both sides, either "Love sure" "Sure love." I can't remember how that started. Something about a typo.

I wrote to him and visited him in any number of places: Belize, San Francisco, Pacific Grove, Irvine (where he taught at the University of California for a couple of semesters, until they got weary of trying to decide whether he could be budgeted under Creative Writing, History or Philosophy), Bend, Oregon. Norfolk, Virginia (that was the brief stay at Old Dominion College—no one ever *did* figure how to budget for Avram), Snohomish, Washington. Fort Lewis, Washington, where he'd been hospitalized on suspicion of being clinically depressed. "Clinical, shminical. You're poor, you're old, you're alone, this gets depressing. What clinical?"

Where else? Port Orchard, Washington—right, that was the veterans' home, where a lifetime of books, notes and correspondence had somehow to be crushed into one room. I don't know how he did it, or what was lost, only that he did it.

Once, hunting for him there, I found him in a sort of common room, empty except for himself and a three-quarters-mad old man who was carrying on a mumbly monologue, to do—I *think*—with the inadequacy of his disability allotment, and the Pentagon conspiracy responsible for it. Avram listened and listened, and shook his head occasionally in wonder at human wickedness, and wouldn't leave with me until the old man had finally nodded his permission. That's another way I remember him: courteous beyond the call of duty, and always when you least expected it.

I helped him move once, in San Francisco. Not his body, but— far more essential to him—his *boxes*, those incredible cartons of manuscripts, files, notebooks, index cards, and what Avram called "the Vergil Matrix," containing absolutely everything known or conjectural concerning Roman civilization in the first century BC. (He got two classic novels—*The Phoenix and the Mirror* and *Vergil In Averno*_out of that research, and left a third, *The Scarlet Fig*, complete behind him, along with the material for how many more...?) It all had to go into storage—nothing new for those boxes—which involved a lot of driving back and forth and, inevitably, a lot of trudging up hills and stairways. Avram was immaculately dressed for the occasion (tweeds, yet, God save the mark!), never complaining or seeming even to break a sweat. But he walked very slowly, because of the gout and arthritis, and it was a long day's work.

At the end of it, sitting over dinner in a Clement Street restaurant, I said, "*Reb* Davidson Sahib, has it ever occurred to us to apply for such a thing as a grant? A fellowship, like?"

Those eyebrows lumbered upward. "Would *you* give such as me a grant?"

"Like a shot. You'd be the first on the list." I considered. "Mmm. Do I have a board of directors?"

"There's always a board of directors," Avram said. "Thank you all the same, but I don't fill out those things anymore. When one doesn't bother to graduate from places, when one's books are mostly paperbacks with titles like *Mutiny in Space, Rogue Dragon* and *Clash of Star-Kings* and one's scholarly testimonials all come from unlicensed pulp-fiction types like your esteemed self □ well, one pays, that's all. Not for dinner, I would hope, but for one's choices. Pass the tartar sauce, *effendi*, and I will tell you how it acquired its misleading name."

I passed the tartar sauce. I said, "My parents used to get *Commentary* long ago, before it turned into the *Wall Street Journal*. I remember coming across a story by a certain A. Davidson. That was you?"

"Indeed. My lone little fling with Liddychoor. Very embarrassing for both of us—we look away when we pass each other on the street. No, no, don't waste your time putting me up for all those academic pretties. I don't regret my choices. I've come a long way for a former fish-liver inspector."

But his admirers doggedly went on proposing him for grants, awards, any kind of stipend at all—Vonda N. McIntyre, me, the late Alan E. Nourse (Avram's most loyal friend and unofficial physician), and lord knows how many others. I can't recall that any of our recommendations were ever acknowledged.

Bremerton, Washington. That was the last stop, the basement apartment where Avram and his arthritis waited it out together in a wheelchair, almost utterly dependent upon the varied caretakers to whom his veteran's benefits entitled him. I remember a little neighbor boy who trotted in and out in the most matter-of-fact way, sprawling on the floor to draw pictures, and generally treating that dank dump like an extension of his own home. In a movie (a *European* movie, of course; who else would make a film about a brilliant writer dying in poverty and neglect?) he'd turn out to be the Angel of Death; but he really was just a small boy who'd adopted Avram on the basis of some unspoken agreement between them. I saw that happen several times with Avram and children.

The last time I saw Avram—he died in 1993, two years after I left the Pacific Northwest—there was a typewriter on his lap, and paper in the typewriter. "Ballast. Keeps me from sliding out of the chair." Like a lot of Avram's jokes, it was no joke at all, not since the mini-strokes had begun tearing him away from himself. But I mention this one because that typewriter *was* ballast, and I think it kept him in this tough world long after anything else could have done so. And that's why you happen to be holding this strange and remarkable book in your hands.

The Boss in the Wall is, in most ways, exemplary Davidson, especially in the marvelous meshwork of *faux-* scholarship that only Avram could have so gradually, patiently woven: building on purported fragments of secret researchers, snatches of historical speculations, hints of dogged hidden pursuits, and learned cross-references to all manner of presumably documented world folklore, all to construct a dazzling snare of what is presently designated "magical realism." Avram was doing this sort of thing before Gabriel Garcia Marquez or Umberto Eco; before anybody called it anything but science fiction.

But this novel is atypical of Davidson in one major respect: it is a truly terrifying story. Not that Avram couldn't be frightening when he chose—witness "Where Do You Live, Queen Esther?" or "The Unknown Law," not to mention that time-bomb of a Jack Limekiller tale, "Manatee Gal, Won't You Come Out Tonight?" But pure wet-your-pants terror wasn't ever what Avram was after —more's the pity for his bank account, because he could have written the Kings and the Koontzes into another line of work altogether. *The Boss in the Wall* is a genuine nightmare, and I'm not at all surprised to learn from Grania Davis (Avram's former wife, occasional collaborator, literary executor and splendid, tireless editor) that it was in fact began as one of Avram's dreams. If he ever wrote anything remotely like this one, I never saw it.

But I may yet. Given the contents of those well-traveled boxes, I doubt very much that *The Boss in the Wall* is the last book of Avram's we'll ever have. In fact, a collection of his mystery short stories is due out soon; and there's that third Vergil novel, not to mention that whole astonishing Matrix; and sooner or later someone's bound to collect and publish the Limekiller stories, my own particular favorites. Yet it seems somehow appropriate to me that this one should be the first posthumous Davidson, precisely because it's so deeply different from the Davidson we think we know. If it was Avram's professional curse (and oh, it was) to be unique, the only one of him there ever was, it was also his artistic blessing. We never get to the end of him, and it's a profound comfort to feel that we never will.

STRANGE INHABITANTS AND UNKNOWN BOUNDARIES

by Michael Swanwick

Y ou hold in your hands a small miracle.

By this I mean not the prose of the story—though that is very fine indeed—nor the story itself, though I consider it one of the jewels of a long and distinguished career. I mean simply that this book exists in stark defiance of the laws of probability.

Let me explain.

The idea for *The Boss in the Wall, A Treatise on the House Devil* came to Avram Davidson in a dream sometime in the mid-1980s. Now, it is notoriously difficult to wrest a story from the realm of dreams into the domain of literature. That is because dreams, like reality, are under no obligation to explain themselves. Images and incidents come up out of nowhere to rattle and shake the dreamer, and then return to the sources from which they arose. Dreams that can jolt you awake, bolt upright in the middle of the night, with your heart pounding like a trip-hammer and your eyes wide with terror, will nevertheless resist transition into the logic of the waking world.

Literature, by contrast, requires either an explicit rationale or an implicit reason why there should not be one. Readers want to know Why and How. One way or another, they must be satisfied. Making monsters is easy; the real labor lies in giving them a place to live in the world.

Avram Davidson had a powerful dream, and he set out to harness that power.

He began by writing a sprawling 600-page first draft toward a novel. Unhappily, he was in poor health, and did not have the reserves of energy required to wrestle this unshapely beast into publishable form. So Grania Davis, his former wife and an author in her own right, stepped in to save the project. She went through the material, re-organized it, and wrote up a novel proposal. When this proved insufficient to sell the book, she took over the enormous mass of typescript and set about turning it into a finished novel, polishing and arranging what already existed, and adding new material of her own.

Meanwhile, Davidson was working on a novella version of the story. He worked bits and pieces from Davis' work-in-progress into the novella. New material from the novella made its way into the novel.

Several times, editors expressed interest in either the novel or the novella. But, for all the usual reasons (and as any writer will attest, all the usual reasons are invariably tedious in the telling, so I'll spare you), nothing ever came of it.

The novel version of *Boss* never did make it to a final form. In his later years Davidson came to the conclusion that he was intrinsically a short-story writer, and that his novels were aberrations from the norm, triumphs of labor over natural inclination. Perhaps so. Perhaps it was a project that a young and vigorous Avram Davidson could have easily wrangled into completion. Perhaps not.

We shall never know.

Writing is hard work. Avram, alas, had not the strength. He died with the novella not quite done—complete, but still rough and unpolished.

When a writer dies, friends and family gather up his papers into cardboard boxes and cart them away. Often these papers are offered to libraries; only rarely do the libraries accept them. Some are sold to collectors. Others are packed away (Theodore Sturgeon's were stacked in a closet and the door nailed shut). Most are discarded. This last is the common lot of uncompleted fiction.

Against all likelihood, though—and this really is persistence raised almost to heroism—Grania Davis did not let the decade and some of failed efforts discourage her. She set aside the novel version and, taking some of its best inventions with her, edited the novella into its final form.

It is no longer possible to determine who contributed what to the story. "For sure, the idea, plot, and tone came from A.D.'s original work," Davis writes. But "this has gone through so many drafts and versions and revisions, that it's hard to remember who wrote what."

So the epic ends, with the ship brought safely into harbor, long after most had despaired of its ever being seen again. And its cargo? I called this story a jewel, and I stand by my words. It is a rare thing when a collaborative work can stand among a writer's best. But this is no ordinary collaboration, and Avram Davidson was no ordinary writer.

I hear somebody out there ask, "Well, what made him so special?" and, briefly, I am at a loss for words.

The proper way to enjoy Avram Davidson is simply to open one of his books and let the words wash over you. A true writer is like a force of nature, and however much his work engages the reader on an intellectual level, the essential experience is primal. One loses hold of the exterior world and falls into the prose of the story, into an interior land that looks a great deal like the mind of its creator.

Analysis is necessarily secondary and after the fact.

Avram's interior lands were considerably more spacious and variously stocked than most. They ranged from Atlantis to

Yonkers by way of British Hidalgo, with myriad stops in between. As for their contents □ Davidson was an autodidact, with all that implies. He had "some college," true. But there is no college (alas) that teaches such facts as were his stock-in-trade. And so perforce he became a scholar of the odd and outré, the out of date and unclassifiable, a digger-after-lore and a man who literally knew things that nobody else did.

If you doubt me, look into his delightful *Adventures in Unhistory* (Owlswick Press; introduction by—only the uninformed would call this a coincidence—Peter S. Beagle), a collection of his discursive essays on mandrakes and mastodons, Aleister Crowley and Prester John, the moon and mermaids and mulberry leaves, the Secret of Hyperborea, and very much more. I doubt there is anyone who could read the book through and not stand in awe at the breadth and depth of the man's erudition.

Davidson was what's known as a "prose stylist," which means that if you have a tin ear, you'll find his work unreadable. Just as, if you're tone deaf, you'll go miles out of your way to avoid Beethoven's *Moonlight* Sonata. But for those of us who love the way that words are put together, how they can be made to clash and chime, the hip-hop rhythms of the street and Gregorian sonorities of formal prose, Avram's work is a feast of delights.

Here I must pause, and take a deep breath.

I look back at what I've written about Avram Davidson—worlds, words, facts, kits, cats, sacks—and it's all bits and pieces, like so many gears and watch-cogs deconstructed from a timepiece. Each one is lovely by itself, beautifully shaped, exquisitely polished, wonderfully made. But, examined in isolation, they cannot show you what makes the thing tick.

You'll simply have to read him for yourself.

Davidson was cursed with a great talent, and doubly cursed by his talent being unique. He wrote stories that were beautiful, hilarious, terrifying, and totally unlike anything anybody else has ever written, in a prose that was witty, complex, and a joy to read. Wonderful stories, each one, as a character herein puts it, "a land with strange inhabitants and unknown boundaries."

Such fiction takes longer to craft than simple hackwork, and yet pays no more.

In his lifetime Davidson was widely acknowledged as being something special—a wizard, a shaman, a writer possessed of something perilously close to genius. But because his work was so original, because it did not pleasantly remind people of old and familiar works they'd long ago grown to love, he never derived much financial benefit from it.

Yet for all the poverty he was forced to endure, the recurrent cycles of critical neglect, the difficulties with publishers and editors, the ill health, the novels that would not allow themselves to be written, he never stopped writing. God had given him a special talent; and when you strike a bargain with God, you pay dearly. The Devil, it's true, is a lawyer; but he's only a junior partner in the firm.

Avram kept his end of the bargain.

The Boss in the Wall may well be the last major work we will ever have from the pen of Avram Davidson. Or again, possibly not. I am not privileged to know what strange denizens lurk in the ocean of paper he left behind. In either case, such a gift, years after the author's death, is more—and better—than anything we had a right to expect.

Somewhere, in our imaginations if nowhere else, there must surely be a library containing those works which ought to exist but for one reason or another do not. In its Classics section are preserved the lost epics of the Trojan cycle, most of Greek drama, and the complete histories of Tacitus. In Poetry you can read the poem of which Coleridge's "Kubla Khan" is but a fragment. In Mathematics you can peruse Pythagoras' own texts, and marvel at Ramanujan's mature work. And so on.

The room containing Science Fiction and Fantasy is relatively small, but it holds such treasures as Philip Jose Farmer's original version of *Riverworld*, Hope Mirrlees' second novel, and *The Log of the Mustang Sally* by William Gibson. In this section, Avram Davidson has a shelf all his own. It contains Peregrine Tertius, six or seven Vergil Magus novels (the cycle was originally conceived as a "trinity of trilogies"; two books were completed and a third may yet appear), the two books completing the trilogy began with *The Island Under the Earth*, and the collected Jack Limekiller stories. Among others.

But not, for a miracle, *The Boss in the Wall*.

PREFACE

—And he dwelleth in desolate cities,
and in houses which no man inhabiteth ...
Job XV, 28

To say that the office looked dirty and shabby was to say that water looked liquid and wet. Newspapers, documents, magazines, clippings, files and folders lay stacked and slipped and scattered. Someone was thrusting his hand into a large manila envelope. Someone was turning the pages of an old illustrated publication. Someone was going through a scrapbook, moistening loose corners with a small glue-brush. On one webby wall was a sign: THE CONTRACT NEVER EXPIRES. None of the men was working hard or working fast, none of them seemed interested in what he was doing, and whatever they were all doing, they gave the impression of having been doing it for a long, long time.

I
<u>What Larraby's Got</u>

The not-crisp card read:

> Edward E. Bagnell
> Professor of Ethnology
> Sumner Public College

Curator Larraby of the Carolina Coast Museum looked up from the card. "Still sticking to 'Ethnology,' are they?" His tone was civil, even amiable, but there was a something in his eyes beyond the usual mere shrewdness.

"Yes sir, they are. Still sticking to 'Public', also." Bagnell was sure there was something sticking to the Curator's manner, inside the ruddy, well-worn face, lurking around the corners of the well-trimmed gray mustache and the picturesquely tufty silvery eyebrows. The Curator asked a few questions about Sumner Public College: Was Macrae getting on with his study of so-called "Moorish" mountain people? Was SPC having the usual small-college trouble with trustees who wanted more money spent on football than on music, say, or scholarship—*real* scholarship? Then there was a pause, and then the odd expression ceased to be odd at all, and was now plain to see.

Slyness.

And with that came the very slow, very quiet, "Well, what can I do for you, Professor Bagnell?"

Out with it.

"I understand that you have a Paper-Man here under lock and

key, Curator Larraby."

At once: "Yes I *thought* that was what you—don't know how I knew, but I—*what did you say?*" The slyness was gone, it was quite gone. The ruddy face was now quite red, the slightly jowly mouth hung agape. "*What* did you say?"

"A Paper-Man or Paper-Doll or Paper-Doll Man. A Hyett or Hetter or Header. A Greasy-Man or String-Fellow. A Rustler or Clicker or Clatterer. And/or other names. Though I assume ... I'm sure you know."

For a moment, silence. Then an audible swallow, a shake, as though the heavy, aging body had been set slightly askew and needed to be set right. A shudder, and then the slumped old man said, "This assumption cannot be allowed to get into the newspapers or the newsreels. This ..."

The newsreels! Bagnell had never seen a newsreel, any more than he had ever seen a passenger pigeon or a Civil War veteran. "Oh God no! That's the last thing we would want!"

The effect was galvanic. The curator was on his feet. "I require another name, and then we'll see how sure you are that I know."

Bagnell said, "*The Boss in the Wall.*" Larraby was out the door before Bagnell was finished, but he was waiting in the hall.

"I was, as I said, sure that was what you wanted, young man. Pardon me, Professor. But I figured you'd go about it slyly." The older man put his arm through Bagnell's, and the gesture at once dissipated all mistrust. "I'm taking you to the top of the tower, it's up these stairs, and I may lean on you quite a bit: no elevator. Slowly. Good."

The stairs were swept clean and smelled of old wood and polish, but as they went up higher a strong odor of disinfectant became predominant. "—And if you had, why, I'd have hustled you right out of here. And here's the key, Dr. Bagnell. The *first* key."

Inside the tower was a locked room which required a second key, and inside this was a modern steel cabinet with two keyholes; alongside it stood an open jug of creosol. "Tower door locked behind us? Make sure. Lock this one and swing the night-bolt too. Now, got a strong stomach?"

Bagnell said that he had helped to find and bury hurricane and flood victims. He now noticed another odor in the rather small room, a strong one, entirely different from the tarry reek of the disinfectant.

"Had such experience? Well, useful. Don't say it's better, don't say it's worse; different. Clean different." He was gently inserting a key. "But not clean. *God,* no." He looked up, withdrew the key. "Oh, forgot. Got a handkerchief? Put some of that bay rum on it; you may feel that you want it in a hurry." On a small table in the corner was, of all things, a bottle of that once-widely-used gentlemen's lotion and hair-tonic. Bagnell had thought it had gone out with newsreels. Was that the source of the other odor? God, no! Bagnell obediently scattered some spicy bay rum on his handkerchief. Larraby had the second key in and out.

Inside were two perfectly ordinary large cardboard cartons with laundry soap logos on them. "*Two?* I thought there was *one.*"

"Think twice. There is." And so there was.

It was in two pieces.

The trousers and jacket were antique, and dull with dirt and some sort of grease; the words *corpse fat* came swift into Bagnell's mind. On one bony foot, and it was as though the skin had been scraped thin before being replaced over the bones—and the skin was filthy beyond anything he had ever seen before, was a part of something doubtless once a shoe. The jacket was torn; it was worn-torn and it was ripped-torn, and beneath it was part of a shirt. And the shirt-part was worst of all, for it must have once been white. No other color could ever have become so ghastly gray, and here and there were stains of other colors, though none was bright.

"Breathe through your handkerchief, and don't get too close as you lean over it."

Bagnell obeyed. Though not before an accidental breath gave him knowledge of the actual smell. A breath was enough. It was not what he had imagined it might be. The smell was organic, he was sure of that, but it was nothing like any organic—or for that matter inorganic—odor he had ever been exposed to before. It was worse than mere decay or decomposition, worse than any disease, worse— He had covered his nose but he could, even despite the scented distillation of the bay and the thick rank creosol, taste it; he covered his mouth as well.

Pieces of shredding yellowed-filthied paper poked out here and there: from under the ragged ankle-edge of the trouser cuff. From out of the gap where the fly had been, the tattered paper protruded like a codpiece. Worn and stained paper formed a sort of ghastly lace jabot high in front. And all of it that he could see showed awful and ugly stains, and even some of the stains had stains.

Larraby took up an exceedingly long pair of rather odd tongs and turned the upper torso half-over; it must have been very light for him to do it with one hand. "Look there." There was an immense hole beneath the left shoulder-blade. And it had been stuffed, there was no other word for it, stuffed with paper.

Larraby said, through his own handkerchief mask, "Of course we never attempted to examine all the paper, but I can inform you that it seems to consist mostly of the special election supplement of the *New York Herald* of November whatever-it-was, 1864, which proves nothing; old Greeley shipped his weekly edition all over the country."

Bagnell's eyes were darting here and there, noting the clawlike hand encrusted with far more than a century's (perhaps) filth, noticing the rubbed-out part of the sleeve from which protruded a something grimy and grim which was likely an elbow. Noticing ... *not* noticing—

"The head's not there."

"Oh." Bagnell's eyes were again darting.

"The head's not *here*, is what I mean. Don't bother looking for it. Seen enough?"

Bagnell thought he'd probably seen enough.

"But I've got a photograph of it downstairs." And Larraby went to locking up the cabinet. Then Bagnell let them out. Then Larraby locked up behind them.

"A photograph of—?"

"—Of the head. Want to know what the fellow said? Fellow who brought the body to us? Do, eh? A' *right!*—Steady; going down is not so easy for me as some might think. —Said he saw *it,* that thing upstairs, saw it lying on the floor of ... a certain old building. Said he saw a rat scuttle over and start to gnaw at one of its feet. Said—you ready for this? *A'right,* said he saw the thing catch the rat with its *foot*—the *thing's* foot. Said he saw it jerk the rat up and heard the rat squeal. Ever hear a rat give a death-squeal when some gant old tiger-she-cat with a dirty kitten catched hold of it? And he said that thing, old Boss-Devil, began to eat the rat. That dried up old horror, supposedly dead a hundred years, with flesh as sere as a mummy's, *began to eat the rat.* Could it happen? *God,* no! Did it happen? *God,* yes!"

As for the head; it was a good photo.

The mouth was still mostly full of teeth, visible beneath the writhed-up lip, and seemed to Bagnell very capable of clicking and clattering—and perhaps—of killing a rat ... a very large rat, too. The nose was sunken but was by no means gone. Something had happened to one ear—how many times might it have offered itself as bait for rats, if rats were what it wanted; lying on rotting floors in rotting buildings by moonlight or in moondark, in forgotten tumuli behind now-vanished pest-houses? —Something had happened to one ear and one eye was closed—but one eye wasn't. It was likely no more than a trick of the light, but the eye seemed to be looking watchfully out of one squinted corner. The eye seemed to have a very definite expression and seemed (as such things often will) to be looking directly at Bagnell, who did not in any way like the look. It was not what Bagnell would think of as fearful. The look was ... what?

Sly.

He shuddered. Curator Larraby, once again just another on-the-way-to-being-old man said, somewhat smugly, "Ah. Now it catches up with you. Here. Something I keep on hand, case of snake-bite. Have one with you." After the first sip, the second sigh, the curator said, "Save you the trouble of asking. No, you may not have a copy. Want a photograph of the head, direct you to Dr. Selby Abott Silas, scholar, rogue and thief, and most unworthy damned

Yankee rat and rascal, holder of the magniloquent title of Principal Steward of the General Museum of the Province of Rhode Island and Providence Plantations. Details on request. Some other time. Further questions? Brief ones …"

As Bagnell made a last and fruitless look towards the flat and locked steel box with the photo of the Paper-Man's head, and made to go, one further question came to him.

Larraby made no objection to answering. The man who had brought in the thing upstairs, in two pieces plus the head, brought them in a gunny sack; the man was a well-known manslayer. "Had killed two Negroes, well, was *tried* for two. Half-black, half-Catawba Indian; a Mustee, we used to call them. And after he'd done a year or so in the penitentiary, where by the way he behaved himself, and I'm sure no one stole his cigarettes or tried to commit a crime against nature upon him, ho no! Well, while he was away there'd been some breakage here, theft and vandalism, so we pulled some strings, got Mustee a parole by offering him the job of second night-watchman; midnight to eight a.m. He looks like *Australopithecus maledictus*, and you may be sure that no one comes around here now who's got no lawful business. Mustee has no morals, no religion, feared of *nothing*, keeps his contracts. Gave him one hundred silver dollars for his find, and a big bottle of over-proof rum. —Hm, maybe I'll give Mustee a ticket to Providence, Rhode Island. Hm, think about it." Larraby thought about it as he reached for a lamp.

"Let me put some more lights on. Old newspapers, yes, indeed. Keep out the cold, they do. Wonder what *you*'ll do, next time you hear a rustle in the dark. *Your* life has been changed forever. Well, nobody twisted your arm; you can always sell insurance. Mind your step on your way out."

"How did Mustee kill those two, ah, Negroes?"

Larraby, winding a light scarf, looked at him eye to eye. "Broke their necks," he said. "Quote me for one single word in print about this, I'll ruin your career without compunction."

And that was the first time Bagnell actually saw one.

So he informed his friend, Dr. Claire Zimmerman, when he called her later that day. In the past that call would have been heralded by the almost-necromantic words: This is Long Distance Calling. But neither of them remembered that, and neither had seen a newsreel. The past was sending them different messages … far more distant and dangerous.

* * *

Excerpt From the Interim Committee Report:

"How many appearances, or maybe we should say sightings, have been reported, would you say?" asked Branch.

"Don't know," said Bagnell.

"Define your terms," said Claire Zimmerman. "How reported, to whom reported?"

"Well, it should be possible to find out. That would help combat it, wouldn't you think?" asked Branch. "Do we even know, for instance, how many authenticated cases there are of one of them doing actual bodily harm to a human being?"

"How authenticated, by whom authenticated? Oh, there are accounts, sure. Bite wounds and scratches, mostly, and talk of festering and amputations," said Bagnell. "We just don't *know.* We think the Boss in the Wall is scaring us. Maybe he thinks we're scaring him. How many of them are there? We don't know. Do they know we're on to them and that we're after them? Can they communicate with each other? Do they? We don't know. Are they suffering from some kind of unknown virus, and if so, is the disease still spreading? Has it infected and infested some of the filthy derelicts we see lying in the doorways of old buildings? Are the drifters sliding and sickening and deteriorating into Paper Men? We don't know. What's it all about—and what can we really do except burn down every old house in the country?"

II
The Old House

T he new house was very old, and Elsa Beth Smith and Professor Vlad Smith loved it at once.

Partly they had come to see it because of the cottage cheese fight of the people next door, and partly it was because of Uncle Mose, that fine old rogue.

College Residence Building Number Three had been, like all Bewdley College's new Residence Buildings, military housing during the war. *The* War; World War Two. "A duplex!" was Elsa Beth's first exclamation on entering her and Vlad's new home—a brave cry which ignored the stained walls, leak-marked ceilings, pokey kitchen, and warping walls and doors and window frames. The buildings had not been built to last. They were, in fact, *not* lasting, they were decaying fast, but people still lived in them all the same. And among the people were the people next door, Professors Albert and Anna Murray, husband and wife. The Murray marriage was not going too well, and a hearty sneeze penetrated the thin partition between the two families.

"Smell this,"—Anna Murray coming out on the porch.

"Throw it out,"—Albert Murray, nose in paper.

"Throw out a whole carton of cottage cheese?"

"Don't throw it out then, *dammit!*" Albert bellowed.

Inside their house, Vlad and Elsa Beth's four-year-old daughter Bella says softly, "Abbert and Amma are fighting again." A slight and sallow child, resembling her father. Not precocious. She has her ways, what child has not? And the mere way she has of standing in a doorway with a wry, dry look on her small face makes her parents wonder how the doorway ever existed before Bella came to stand in it.

Her parents do not directly reply. They consider their options. "The rents in quaint old Bewdley City are out of sight," sighs Elsa. She was once a strawberry blonde, but since Bella was in utero, Elsa's hair has darkened to a light brown. Her face, with its slight suggestion of a double chin, looks very thoughtful. She is a talented painter and she is very nice.

Not long thereafter came Uncle Mose's letter.

Uncle Mose wrote: "Moses Stuart Allenby is looking around for a sponge to throw in. I am tired of robbing widows and orphans, and I'm going to make you kids an offer. Elsie Bessey knows I'm quiet and clean in my habits. Mostly I sit in my room studying subversive publications like *The Wall Street Journal,* play a little jazz on my gramophone, take walks and watch birds. Want to relax at home, but must have a home, and have no desire to sleep on your sofa. So here's the offer: All around small towns are perfectly suitable houses which never appear on any real estate lists because they are too old and unfashionable. Beware of Grecian pillars, cost another fifty thou and who needs them? Here are the magic words: *A quick sale for $25,000 cash.* Your local land agent will blench and swallow nervously. Then he will run around like a roach in rut season. You'll be surprised how fast he comes up with something usually thought unsaleable. Old, old houses are solidly built or they wouldn't have survived to be old, old. Uncle Mose was a farm boy, built and repaired many a barn and old house before leaving on the milk train to the city. Uncle Mose will leave love-birds alone to bill and coo, and will often baby-sit little Bella, teach her to play poker and dance the hootchie-cootchie."

✳ ✳ ✳

"There's the house, Professor, to the right," said realtor Bob

Barker with a toothy smile.

The words formed in Vlad's mind: *That house wasn't even built in the 19th century.* He saw a small replica of Andrew Jackson's Hermitage, with squared wooden pillars, lacking even a lick of plaster, holding up the verandah's second story. Not Grecian at all —just an old, old house that George Washington never slept in.

"Let's go in, if you folks are ready," Bob Barker said. They were ready. "Got to tell you honestly that this house is almost devoid of your modern conveniences. No electricity, no telephone, but no problem there, the lines run right past the place. It's well-water, but the pump is inside the house. There is just merely one bathroom, and it empties into a cesspool. Watch out for the far end of the porch, got a rotten place there." The key kept in a niche in the sill was modern. That was perhaps the only thing which was.

"I love it, I love it," said Elsa Beth. "I love it, I love it," said she.

Uncle Mose came two days later.

"My *God,* Uncle Mose," said Vlad, "what is that you've got with you?" It was gray with reddish lights in its pelt, and it was huge, and it panted at them and lolled its tongue. "It's big as a cow!"

Bella said, "*That's* no cow, that's a *big dog.*"

"You're right, little Belly. A St. Hubert hound named Nestor. Fine with kids, but burglars watch out! Where's some iced tea? Where's our new house? Settle down Mose," he advised himself. Moses Stuart Appleby had been rather tall and his shoulders still hinted at broadness. He was, as always, immaculate. "I'm all packed and weighed and ready for freighting, soon as I'm sure. Ready to go? *I'm* ready to go. Let's fill a big thermos with iced tea, Elsie Bessy."

They stopped in town for him to mail a letter, and an aged black man rose to confront them in clothes washed threadbare-clean. "You the folks buyin' ol' Rustler house nigh the river?"

"Was that its name, Russel? I didn't know that," said Vlad. "It's on old River Road, though. Yes."

The old man nodded. His skin was gray and his eyes were glazed with age. "That's it. I born here, call me Pappa John. Can I pleased to give you folks some kindly advice? They is three warnings.

Firstly, get you a cat. They *hates* cats. Nextly, keep you a fire. They *feared* o' fire. And lastly, please folks, *never* get between one o' *them* and the *wall*." He nodded his ancient head. Vlad, understanding not one word, thanked him and went on into the post office. And then the town sped by ...

"There it is."

Uncle Mose looked and said nothing, until they went up on the wide verandah which ran all around the house. "Hey, look there. A tree. A lilac tree. Some old-time housewife planted a lilac bush, and now it's grown taller than the house. Well, let's open her up."

Faint broom tracks showed that some attempt at house-cleaning had been made more recently than the planting of the lilac bush. Faint tremors and echoes in the old, old house. How old? Maybe in the title-deed. Maybe not. Were the Russels that old Pappa John mentioned the original owners? What was Uncle Mose doing? Uncle Mose was leaning over with his ear against the wall. Catching Vlad's questioning eye, he gestured for Vlad to do the same. At first Vlad heard something like the sound of the sea in a sea-shell. After that came fainter and odder sounds. A rustling ... a far-off clicking.

A breath lightly brushed his neck and Vlad jumped. It was Uncle Mose. "Hear anything?"

"Rats, maybe."

"Rats don't rustle. Rats don't click. We'll put out some rat-traps, then we'll see."

Attempts, rough and rude enough, had been made to keep the old house in order. In one room the ancient roses of the wallpaper bloomed faintly, almost evoking a ghostly perfume. Elsewhere the walls were papered only with yellowing, tattered newspaper. In one large closet, "Whew, kind of musty in here," said Vlad.

"Whew is right. Worse than that."

"Dead rat under the floorboards, or inside the wall?"

Uncle Mose shrugged. "Old houses, Lord, how they retain. Maybe the moldy diapers of a baby who died a hundred years ago. Well, no problem. Open all the doors and windows, have the place scrubbed down from attic to cellar.

* * *

Back home, and effusively greeted by the great hound Nestor, and by Bella fresh and pink-cheeked from her nap. They had drinks. They discussed the house. They all agreed they loved the house. Discussion had reached a pleasantly high level when there was a piercing scream.

Tonight at the Murrays' it was Anna's turn to scream.

Vlad hastened to speak. "Say, why don't we have a cook-out somewhere? A picnic?"

"Oh, good!" said Elsa. "Hey! Why don't we have it at the new house?" Then Elsa had her great and wonderful idea: "Why don't we *sleep* out there tonight in sleeping bags? To celebrate, I mean."

"All in favor, say Aye," directed Uncle Mose, and he insisted that everything was to be his treat. And they got lots of everything.

* * *

At the old house: "The steaks are doing just fine," said Uncle Mose. "I want to check something out. Bring some flashlights and come along." He walked into the house with long strides, and what he wanted to check out was soon revealed. "Nothing in this trap, nothing in that one. Let's take a look in the cellar … nothing. Traps are clean as a whistle. As near as I can see, there isn't a rat in the whole place."

Elsa said, of course, that she was delighted to hear it. "And I'm pleased to see how thick the walls are. It'll stay cooler in the summer and warmer in the winter. My mother always said that high ceilings and thick walls are healthy."

Nestor moved his huge head delicately. Nestor had been doing his own checking-out, and was still alert.

Bella said, "This is our new house." The grown-ups were pleased. Yes, they said, this was their new house. Without changing her slow and level tone, Bella said, "I don't like it." Then she repeated, "I don't like it." Nor did she say any more.

When the steaks were ready, they took their seats on the front steps. The steaks were tender and very, very good.

Later, upstairs in the rose-papered room, sleeping bags side by side, Elsa said, "You know, for an old bachelor, my uncle knows a thing or two. The gentle way he convinced Bella to share the downstairs room tonight, without a single protest. He must know this is a sort of special honeymoon thing. You and me."

Vlad did not immediately answer. He rolled over so his sleeping bag slightly overlapped hers. "Your place or mine," he whispered.

Afterwards, Vlad went down to use the antique toilet behind the stairs. The door of one room opened a crack; lamplight and shadow. "Vlad?" said Uncle Mose.

The door opened wider. The great St. Hubert hound appeared, his master close behind. "Would you be kind enough to let Nestor out the front door for a minute? Same errand as you. Let him back in when you're ready. Didn't want to leave Bella alone in case she woke up, first time in a strange house."

"Sure. Let's go, Nestor." The dog came forward, gave Vlad a sociable sniff, waited until the front door was opened, and ambled off into the night. Vlad turned back, flashlight in hand, toward the water closet under the stairs.

"Oh, by the way, Uncle Mose; that funny sound we heard that time, when we were listening at the wall? The rustling and, uh, clicking? I heard it again a few minutes ago, when I happened to have my ear against the floor."

"Look into it in the morning. On about your business now, your wife might be nervous alone upstairs. G'night." The older man nodded, retreated into his chamber. Those two words were the last ones Vlad would ever hear him clearly say.

The plumbing rushed and gurgled loudly. Vlad stood by to make sure the ancient equipment suffered no overflowing; then went to the front door. Nestor appeared at once. "Good boy." Light still showed beneath the closed door of Mose's room.

Then the things began to happen.

In what order did the things happen? Some things happened simultaneously, and there was no time to pause and think. The first thing was absolutely astonishing in itself. Nestor flung himself into the air, absolutely vertically; his feet even left the floor. Then he hurled himself, still upright, against the closed door with the crack of light beneath it. Before his immense body slammed against the door, Bella began to scream in a thin and terribly high tone which Vlad had never heard from her before. At once there was an answering scream from Elsa upstairs and, more or less at the same time, Nestor's body slammed against the door. Uncle Mose roared and his feet ran, tramping, inside the room which had gone dark. Nestor howled and tried to break down the door. Vlad flung himself upon the door, and fell against Nestor instead. He tried to hold his light steady to see and grasp the door knob.

Still Nestor howled, still the old man stumbled inside the closed room, and still Bella screamed. —And the door opened and Vlad staggered into the room and tried desperately not to lose his balance. The noises Uncle Mose made were not roars any longer; Uncle Mose it was who staggered, lurched, fell upon his back and rolled to his side. Bella had stopped screaming, and was utterly silent. Nestor flung himself across the room and the house shook.

Elsa came screaming in, and then she did absolutely the worst thing she could possibly have done—and somehow Vlad knew absolutely that she was going to do it. She seized the arm of the hand in which he held the flashlight, and she tugged down on it as she called her daughter's name, and the flashlight swung wildly up and down until he managed to get it into the other hand.

Nestor was throwing himself against the wall and clawing at the wall, howling and slathering, and something fell from his mouth. Vlad reeled as he tried to dislodge his wife and to focus the flashlight. Then Elsa let go of Vlad's arm and ran to pick up her child, who was arching and thrashing and kicking and making sharp howling sounds. Elsa picked her up, but Bella's arms and legs still moved and jerked convulsively.

What else was in the room? Something else had been in the room.

Someone else had been in the room. Something … someone filthy and frightful and foul had been in the room.

There to one side was the Coleman lamp, and Vlad forced himself to calm his hands and to relight the lamp, and the room filled with hissing light. No one else and nothing else was in the room now.

Still the huge dog flung himself against the wall. Then it stopped.

Bella stopped her frightful convulsions. She hung limp in her mother's arms, even when Elsa had fallen on her knees onto the sleeping bag, pressed her ear against the tiny chest, lifted her horrified face to him and nodded slightly.

Nestor stepped delicately on huge feet to his master, nuzzled him and licked him, and began to utter a deep and moaning lament. Was the old man dead? Vlad slowly got down beside the body and said, "Uncle Mose? Nestor? Uncle Mose?" Slowly he placed his ear against the fallen man's chest. There was no rustling sound he heard, no clicking. He heard no sound at all. Nestor sniffed again and began to howl.

* * *

The long, slow, cold nightmare continued. Call the police, deputy sheriffs, sheriff's deputies. The hospital: "Well, it's shock, basically. Your little girl is of course the most affected, but your wife too is in shock. I'm afraid you aren't in too good shape yourself."— Take these … sign these … tell us again, Professor, exactly what happened: questions asked by the doctors and by the police.

Shock, Professor. Your only child has ceased to be a little girl who stood in a doorway and turned your heart with a single look. She became a wind-up doll which screamed and thrashed, except when the doll wound down and looked dully out of unfocused eyes. *Shock, to use simple language, short-circuits the nervous system.*

"What did she see that caused this shock? What sort of creature, sir? It is difficult for us to believe, you see, because your wife doesn't report anything like that. Don't be offended, sir, but you too have suffered a severe shock of some sort ..."

"What the hell, Branch, what the hell?"

Vlad's old friend, and fellow Professor of Folklore David Branch looked at him and said, "Nobody knows what the hell, Vlad. We have to take this one step at a time."

"Why was Uncle Mose's funeral and cremation over so quickly ... why was his collar so high?" Then another thought sprang into Vlad's mind. "Where's Nestor?"

"He's at Dean Jorgenson's farm; it's in the next county, so the sheriff can't get him to shoot."

"*What*? Why would they shoot Nestor?"

"Well, mainly because they were afraid of him. This great brute was leaping around, terribly upset, and next thing a deputy got the idea that, well, maybe Nestor had killed the old man— Impossible? Why, impossible?"

"I told them the dog wasn't *in* the room ... when it began to happen."

"Well, they didn't know that and, um, I heard that Mose had some sort of *marks* on his throat that might have killed him so— Anyway, Nestor ran off and Dean Jorg heard about it, and called the trembling beast into his van and drove him across the county line, so Nestor's all okay. What next?"

"I want to go back to that dammed old house ... and I need some plastic bags."

At the supermarket, leaning on the back of a superannuated cart containing aluminum cans, empty bottles, and odds and ends of light junk was someone whom Vlad recalled meeting. Remembrance was mutual. Stopping his wagon, the old black man said, "I sorry, sir, about you daddy." Why bother with a correction? Vlad nodded, sighed. "Must be you daddy fo'get, done git between it and the wall ... fine ol' gentleman."

Vlad stared. Remnants of thought came whirling by, as if caught in a gale. "What do you mean, Pappa John? Get between what and the wall ... what wall?"

The age-glazed eyes in the furrowed face looked at him. "Them bad things as we finds sometimes in old houses. Them Rustlers or Clickers ... them Paper-Men. The *Boss*, sir, the Boss in the Wall. How the lady and the lee girl? *The Boss done stole the lee girl's soul and you gots get it back.*"

He pushed off, leaving Professor Branch looking after him, leaving Vlad with his mouth twitching. "Did you understand what old John meant, Branch?"

"I believe I do, which is not to say that I believe it as facts."

"I should tear that damned house apart ... find evidence."

They drove beyond the small town and along the country road. The old house looked far different in late afternoon sunshine than it had at night. In the room where Uncle Mose and Bella had cheerfully agreed to spend the night lay a well-worn red rubber toy.

Vlad pointed out to Branch a portion of the wall deeply and recently scored by talons. "Those are Nestor's claws, I guess." He put his ear against the wall; heard nothing. "It's hollow," he said.

"It would be. Proves nothing by itself."

Vlad abruptly said, "Ah, that's what I came for." He pointed to something in the corner. "It was in her hand, and she dropped it when I picked her up." He took the plastic bags out of his pocket.

Branch knelt and looked, then he sniffed. This time it was his face that writhed. "Paper. It looks like old newspaper ... well, this is an old house. What a godawful stench. You say it was in your wife's hand?"

"No, it wasn't my wife," said Vlad, as he carefully used one plastic bag to scoop the object into another. "It was my daughter who had it clutched in her hand. It was Bella."

No further search could legally be made of the house, and no walls would be torn apart. According to the sheriff's department, the deceased died from a stroke or a heart attack, possibly following an attack by a dog or some other animal. Case closed.

❋ ❋ ❋

At the hospital, Elsa woke up and took a light supper, then she slept again. Bella's condition was unchanged. Elsa's aunt, Uncle Mose's sister, invited them to stay at her big house in the country after they were released. Elsa softly told Vlad that she thought the change would do her and Bella good. Vlad reluctantly agreed.

"Jesus, Branch, what should I do?" said Vlad when they returned to College Housing. "It is my belief that Uncle Mose died of a severe bite in the throat by some sort of degenerate or derelict creature, for lack of better words, and that's what terrified my wife and daughter, and messed up our lives. That's what I told the doctors and the sheriffs, and nobody believed me. No autopsy was done before his body was cremated, and ..."

"Do? Well the first thing to do is take Doctor Branch's prescription of a big drink of whatever booze you have on hand, and then you are going to lie down and pretend to sleep. I will put on some sleepy-type music and ... ah, I'd like to look through your files. I promise not to read any love notes or old paternity warrants; I want to look for learned matter. Folkloric shop stuff, okay?"

Pretending to sleep was, as expected, succeeded by genuine slumber. Then by awakening and finding Branch reading by lamplight. "What's that you're reading, Branch?"

"I thought you'd never ask." He tilted up an old red folder mended with tape. "Look familiar?"

Vlad felt that it did look familiar, that he knew what was in it, and somehow he did not *like* what was in it. He recalled a small voice saying, "Is this our new house? I don't *like* it." He leaned his head on his hand and choked back tears.

Branch shoved the folder over to Vlad, who slowly opened and leafed through it. What was this on yellowed paper, laboriously typed in old-fashioned typescript? *Transcript of Alleged Rare Pamphlet Allegedly Entitled "The Treatise on the House Devil."* And this: a sheaf of sundry papers, typed and penned and machine-copied on various sorts of copy machines, attached by a large rusting paper clip, and labeled *Bagnell's Notes.* An item caught his eye; *Preliminary Survey of the Folklore of Two Ohio River Tributaries:* "I had the usual difficulties: first you must find your source. Then you must make him talk. Then you must make him stop talking. Or her. In fact it was from a her that I learned a folk remedy for pubic lice which is too gross for learned journals. Also I heard the following account which might interest you: Near a place called Wide Waters, where two large boats could pass each other, was a tower. It was originally as tall as a three-story building, but then kind of crumbled. Some say it was used as a shot-tower or a lighthouse. Others say it was built by a wicked Frenchman to remind himself of France. He was cruel to his slaves and nearly starved them to death. Well, as soon as Lincoln freed the slaves, they mixed up a big batch of cement and carried over a big pile of stones, and walled their evil old master—their *Boss*—inside the tower. Then all the former slaves ran off. There were no windows in the tower, just little slits. And before anybody came around and found him, long after he must have died, they say he got so thin he was able to poke his hands through the slits and wave them around. And they say you can still sometimes see the skeletal hands of the cruel 'Boss in the Wall' waving through the slits on stormy nights.

"You can recognize elements of countless Old World legends of cruel leaders walled in towers, such as the Sultan of Baghdad and the Mouse Tower on the Rhine. Though the skeletal hands waving through the slits may be strictly a local touch."

"Okay, Branch, okay. I got it now; I remember," Vlad wept. "Why didn't I remember it before?"

Branch had poured moderate drinks for both of them from a bottle, sipped his own and gestured to his old friend to do the same. "Here's a possible explanation. Why did you originally forget it? Because you *forgot,* that's why. Who the hell remembers everything? Every wife in the world feels compelled to shove some of her husband's old crap out of sight, and you had other things to do, so you forgot. Then you went to the old house, and just the sight of the place, or some little sound or smell started to bring back memories. But you didn't *want* the memories. You and your wife and uncle wanted the old house, and the memories weren't very nice. So your mind suppressed them. Until that moment. Let's say that your uncle had some kind of stroke, or fit of convulsions. He couldn't breathe, so he clawed and tore at his own throat. Suppose your daughter woke up and saw him, and she started to scream and scream." Branch took another sip and continued, "Suppose that what you saw was so terrible, your mind couldn't admit that you saw it. You *had* to be seeing something else. Your mind, so to speak, *slipped* down, down into the sub-basement. And down there in the mud and jumble, your mind found something. It found those old tales that old Pappa John had babbled about, and it *substituted* those old terror-tales for the terrible thing you were really seeing. All of this in an instant, of course, but the memory lingers on. Maybe your little girl's defense was to retreat into convulsions and unconsciousness."

Vlad groped for words. He felt as if he were on the edges of a deep, dark wood. "Is that what you really think happened? That my buried memories of all those damned old legends made me think I saw ..."

From outside the dark woods came a deep sigh. "That's certainly one explanation, and I advise you to consider it," said Branch, tossing down the rest of the whiskey.

❋ ❋ ❋

Later, much later, Vlad's breath came softly and regularly from the couch. Branch slipped silently out of the room, took up the telephone, and walked as far into the kitchen as its long cord would allow. He turned on the light and a water tap, then dialed a number. Waited.

"Doctor Edward Bagnell, please. Hello, Ed? This is Branch. Yes, I know what time it is. Have a pen and paper? Okay, listen carefully. The House-Devil, Paper-Man, Boss in the Wall; well, I want to report another sighting."

III
Vlad's Quest

How sweetly the small old town smelled in the early summer rains. It seemed to smell of cedar and citronella and water and mint.

Annie Jenkins, Dean Jorgenson's housekeeper, said, "Was it one of those *tramps*, one of those *awful* ones? The Lord knows where they come from or why—luckily not often—oh they don't do anything violent, not lately, they don't even *steal*, the ones I'm thinking of. We used to call them Paper-Men when I was a girl, because they put newspapers under their old clothes to keep warm in winter, though why in *summer?* —Don't even steal, which is very odd if you think of it, they being so poor they can't even afford soap or secondhand clothes. Oh those filthy rags. Just the sight of them, oh and the awful smell of them. I asked my husband what *causes* them, every so often you know. Harry said it was 'slum clearance'. Harry says some awful old abandoned building is torn down somewhere, and then those dreadful derelicts have no place to hide, and so they just wander off, they shamble around, and sometimes they turn up *here*. Thank the Lord they don't seem to stay. I have no idea where they go, but they don't stay here. Was it one of those—? And to think of the sheriff accusing that sweet big dog. Why, when you gave him a shirt his old master had worn, Nestor took it to his bed in the barn, laid the shirt on the straw, and rested his head on it all that day."

∗ ∗ ∗

Dean Jorgenson said, tapping his huge hairy fingers on his desk-top, "Well, good, Stewart. I told Vlad he could take the summer off if he took someone with him. I'm glad it's you. He likes you; says you have a good mind and a good sense of humor. Fortunately this is still a private college and I can finagle you some graduate credits, and something out of the special funds without having to justify it to six state legislative committees. Consider that done. And you, in turn, won't let him get morbid and obsessive about ..." He searched for a word, gazed at Jack Stewart with troubled eyes and concluded, "... *it*."

Vlad looked as if he was fairly well recovered from a bad drunk, but Jack knew that if you *looked* it, you weren't recovered at all. It wasn't until they were bedding down for the first night, in a worn-down motel, that Vlad began to loosen up and talk.

"I understand Jorg's going to do some creative bookkeeping, and get you some grad credits. Good. Officially we're going on just another fun folklore ramble," he ran his fingers over his tired face. "Good clean bright stuff; children's jump-rope jingles, Paul Bunyan tales of the lower Appalachians, Old Darky stories about Mr. Buzz*ard*. But unofficially you are going to be my keeper, eh? We, that's *you*, kid, are going to keep *me*, that's me, kid, from getting into anything gamy or gritty. No folkloric spelunking. But no such luck, kid. God bless poor dear old Jorg, but I'm going after such little-known legends as the Clickers, the Rattlers, and I don't mean snakes, I mean the Greasy-Man, Paper-Man, the Boss in the Wall, see?"

Jack Stewart ran his own fingers through his molasses-colored curly hair, murmured about a shower, looked up and asked, "Why?"

"Why? Because I saw a specter haunting an old house, and it killed my uncle and sent my little girl into convulsions and my wife into a deep depression and, my god, it was *awful*! *Why* was it there? What *was* it, what *is* it? Nobody believes that I really saw it. Hardly anybody in academe even *knows* the legend, let alone believes it. Allbright does. We're going to see Allbright. I've got to find out more about the legend, more about what I saw. I've got to find something that will help my wife and my daughter, help us put our lives back together. Bagnell knows about the legend. We're going to see Bagnell. And ... after that, well, we'll *see*. See?"

Stewart, in turn, liked Vlad's mind and sense of humor. But now he saw a man slumped in unhappiness, confusion, pain. There was much that he wanted to know about what happened. Much he dared not ask, which he knew would be revealed later. So he merely said, "I see."

Vlad kicked off his shoes, rapidly undressed, said he was too tired for a shower. "Have one in the morning. Too tired even to put on the jammies. Maybe I'll put them on in the morning, too. Going to stay up reading? Try the Gideon Bible, Job XV 28, as a starting text. Leave the light on in the bathroom if you like. *Night*."

Jack turned on his reading light. Gideon Bible? Well, there weren't many things you could do in a motel room. Job, huh, XV ... 26, 27, ah .... His finger traced its way to the verse.

28. *And he dwelleth in desolate cities, and in houses which no man inhabiteth ...*

Jack Stewart decided to leave the light on in the bathroom.

❋ ❋ ❋

Robert E.L. Allbright lived amidst the dense green kudzu vines, way away from anywhere, and very far away from the highways. The hand he held out was large and reddened and splotched ... a description of his face, as well. His eyes were red-rimmed and he blinked a lot. "I hope, Professor, that you may have had my letter?" asked Vlad Smith politely. Blink. Blink. "In which I said that I'd like to talk with you about the possible origins of the legends of the Paper-Man, or the Boss in the Wall?" Blink. Blink.

It was not clear if Allbright had led them into his office or his dining room. At one end of a table strewn with books and papers, a late teenaged boy was sitting beside a sort of barricade erected out of old law-books, eating breakfast cereal and milk. "My grandson, Albert S.J. Allbright. In theory he is reading law with me. When he is finished he will be a foremost authority on the foreclosure of mules." His voice had fallen into the flattening tones of the increasingly deaf.

The boy slightly turned his head and raised his hand to it, as though to wipe away Rice Krispies and, looking straight at Stewart said, low-voiced, "You got a joint?"

Stewart opened his mouth to reply, looked at his elders and turned his own head slightly.

The boy got up and shuffled dishes. "Go git you some coffee," he said.

"Give you a hand," said Stewart.

"Well," said Allbright, "I got your letter, where did I put that shoe box?" He rummaged among the many shoe boxes and other things on the table. "Put it—Florsheim Shoes—here." He took up the shoe box, turned it over. A sheaf of typescript settled down on the table. Inasmuch as the width of the average shoe box is somewhat less than that of the average sheet of typing paper, someone had neatly trimmed the papers. The idea had something of the simplicity of genius.

"Here 'tis," Allbright said, "Here 'tis. *A True Account Prepared From The Original Testimony of the Capture and Death of a Paper-Man on the Lands and Domains of Jim Oglethorpre Allbright, Esquire, as edited by his Grandson, Professor Robert E.L. Allbright. With Notes and Commentaries.* —Sorry I don't have a clear copy to give you. Like to look at it?"

"Well," said Vlad, slightly bowled over. "I'd like to … yes … I'd like to talk with you about it. I'd like you to tell me about it, if you don't mind."

Allbright said there was mighty little to tell. "He was located, as my diagram shows, my map here, he was found in one of the old tobacco barns we used to have. And it was set fire to, and he was seen as he ran off, and he was tracked down. My great grandmother was at hand, and she rallied the Negras, and they behaved very bravely, yes sir. My grandfather was at war at the time, and his old mother guarded the fort, so to speak, and gave them courage. Because, generally speaking, they would have fled like deer from such an apparition; who could blame them?"

Who indeed, thought Vlad bleakly.

"As it was, they stoned him with stones until he died."

"*What?*"

Old Allbright slowly nodded his massive, mottled head. "It is what happened, Professor Smith. To be sure." He looked at Vlad directly. "There were skeptics, aren't there always? Some of them said he was a Union prisoner, escaped from Andersonville Prison. Prison *camp,* we would call it nowadays. Some said *that* was why he was so gant. Well, no one denies that Andersonville was very bad. What comes of putting a Dutchman in charge of things. A Switzerdutchman. Starved his prisoners, the scoundrel. Went back to Switzerland during the war, went and returned by running the blockade. How much you want to bet he put a lot of money in one of those banks over there?"

Jack Stewart and the younger Allbright returned, carrying a tray with coffee and mugs, which they set on the table.

"As for the other skeptical account, why, some said that the creature killed was a Confederate deserter who had stripped off his uniform so as not to be identified, and had taken up some rags of old clothes from who knows where, maybe from a farmhouse in the middle of a battlefield. You know there was an old farmhouse right in the midst of the Battle of Bull Run, and an old lady died in that house during the battle, and who knows what went on in there. And as for the creature's gant condition, maybe he hadn't eaten well while he was hiding and skulking. He was discovered in the tobacco barn and tobacco is a filthy weed. I like it, but it's not *nourishing,* which might explain his extreme thinness, and if hunger left him too weak to bathe in a creek, his extreme filthiness —*if* the explanations of the skeptics be true. I have offered this fully documented account to no less than fourteen publications, and would you believe that ten of them decisively declined, and that four did not even reply?”

Jack said, rather abruptly, “If you tell it, sir, I would believe it. Otherwise I would not.”

Vlad also looked surprised. “I should think that such an account of the myth in action would be very acceptable, considering the historical period, and from someone of your stature in the field.”

“My stature in the field. Well, well.” Blink. Blink. His reddened face grew redder yet, but his voice remained flat. “If you had spent as much time in the Groves of Acadeemee as I have, it would perhaps surprise you less.” He poured coffee.

Later in the car Vlad said, “I don’t mind telling you that I was feeling just a bit spooked.”

The kudzu vines sped by, sped by. There seemed to be hardly anybody around, and the few people they saw didn’t seem to be doing anything. Surely they did not, could not, eat the damned stuff.

“Know what you mean,” Jack Stewart said. “What’d you think of that boy, buried alive out here, no wonder he couldn’t think of anything except grass.”

“Well, you can’t smoke kudzu.”

“He said a funny thing, we were sort of rapping about that and this. Well I did most of the talking about old Paper-Man, and he said, ‘You know Larraby’s got one locked up, don’t you?’ And I said, ‘No, who’s Larraby, and what’s he got?’ And then he took a loooong toke, and he said, ‘Well, if you don’t know who Larraby is, then I don’t know what he’s got.’”

Vlad said, “We can ask Ed Bagnell at Sumner Public College.”

And then conversation faded away in the face of endless green tangles of kudzu … kudzu.

* * *

Dr. Edward Bagnell was on the telephone: “Dr. Claire Zimmerman, please. Claire? Ed. Do you have your little slate and pencil there? Okay, listen. On whatsoever excuse, I want you to go to Rhode Island and see Dr. Silas Abbott Selby of the Providence Plantations Museum; this refers to the Paper-Man Project. It's of gross importance and intense confidence; you will go and question Selby about a rumor that he has a Paper-Man's head. *Don't* scream into the phone, for God's sake. Heard it from Curator Luke Larraby of the Carolina Coast Museum, who has Selby in the sights of his Parrott guns—that's confidential. I doubt if one visit will get you a peep, but be prepared to keep at it. It may require a slightly less severe costume and manner; that's up to you. That's all. Kiss, kiss."

Silas Selby had another view of the matter. He sipped Fundador, and looked at Claire over the rim of the glass. Her cropped dark hair framed her round face. They were in the W. Waldo Brown Room, endowed by the philanthropist of that name, some said in order to have a quiet place to drink brandy without his wife.

"Larraby has no training as a museum specialist whatsoever," he said flatly. "He was an architect, and sort of a house doctor for old houses, patching them up, I mean. By and by he began to do work for the old museums down there in Carolina. Well, they were short all kinds of trained people, and he was a quick study, enthusiastic and willing to turn his hand to anything, willing to read up and become the local authority on anything; just the sort of man they needed when the curatorship fell vacant." Selby sipped his brandy, gazed at Claire, and let his eyebrows rise and fall.

"Well, somehow or other Luke had acquired a local mummy. Ante-bellum, post-bellum, or just plain bellum. There are places throughout the world where the soil tends to preserve bodies laid to rest, and such bodies sometimes turned up down Luke's way in places unexpected. I think they became sort of cult objects, who can say why? People went mum when one asked, and people looked at each other out of the corners of their eyes. Local name for them was 'Paper-Men' or 'Paper-Doll,' because the local lovers of grue and ghoulishness had been in the habit of padding their wasted bodies with old newspapers under the clothes, which made them look less gant and skeletal, chests less fallen in, stomachs less shrunken and so on. The ancient Egyptians used small sacks of cedar sawdust for the same purpose, after all. It is reminiscent of old Jeremy Bentham, stuffed and mounted and in his best clothes, attending the annual meetings of the … whichever society. —Now perhaps I should not be telling you all this, Doctor Zimmerman, may I call you Claire? But I feel I can count upon your—?"

He peered at her again over his wine-glass. She assured him (again) that he might count on her.

"More brandy, Miss Zimmerman, or a biscuit? Very well, though I hate to be a solitary drinker." Selby sipped his own. "I was visiting the provincial museums, and had to go about checking it ever so circumspectly. Couldn't come right out and demand to see it. Well, Larraby kept that Paper-Doll thing hidden in a Rinso box in a broom closet! It was in three pieces, in totally deplorable condition. A great troll of a janitor was lurking around. Details shall be spared you. 'Luke, confound it, this should be kept in a moisture and temperature controlled, sealed-case.'"

"Couldn't agree with you more," said Larraby.

"Then why isn't it?"

"Haven't got one, is why. Besides, our fragrant friend might spook the city senseless."

"'And there should be a series of tests made, examinations, measurements, tissue samples. Let me give this some thought.' To make the matter short, a complex plan was worked out. Some recently acquired shekel medallions would be sent to Larraby as sort of hostages, and the head of his precious mummy would be sent north to Rhode Island to be tested, *teeth* for example. Meanwhile I looked into getting a proper sealed case for it. But after a very short time, old Luke Larraby began demanding his, um, object back, and making ridiculous charges that the shekels weren't authentic. Said the shekel medallions, of 18th-century European manufacture, had been represented as actual 2nd-century shekels of the last Jewish Commonwealth, which was certainly not stipulated in the agreement. Said his miserable mini-museum had now provided a more secure repository than the broom closet. Well, the tests take a long time, so Silas Abbott Selby stood firm." The empty glass came down firmly on the table and his eyes firmly held Claire's.

"And I am not likely to yield, my dear Miss, ah, my dear Doctor Zimmerman, for in strictest confidence, there is a great deal of mystery about this whole thing. The tests are inconclusive, but I can disclose that the tests show no traces of such chemical embalming agents as arsenic or formaldehyde or anything more modern. Though what they did disclose was both interesting and puzzling. Certain tissues are inconsistent with ... the state of certain sinew fragments, soft tissue, brain matter and spinal matter, epidermal cells ... but I have no wish to be prolix. Oh, the press would like nothing more, nothing better than to compare us, by 'us' I mean the Carolina Coast Museum and the General Museum of the Province of Rhode Island and Providence Plantations, compare us to Burke and Hare. Ha ha.

"Oh, surely you need not rush away now. A glass of Fundador? Do let me pour you, our Fundador is famous—well, I have very much enjoyed. And should you hear, should you just hear any of, ha ha ha, *Curator* Larraby's, he has no degree in museum science, you know, of his complaints against this ancient and august institution, older than our Republic, well, ha ha, just consider the source. Allow me to help you with your wraps—well, Goodnight, Miss, Doctor Zimmerman. Claire."

In a semi-senile tortoise shuffle came Dr. H. Brown Roberts. "Who was that young woman, Selby? Surely you were not entertaining a personal female guest in these semi-Senatorial chambers, endowed by Uncle Waldo Brown, eh? Looked like a flapper to me. Eh?"

Framed in the arch of the ancient gallery, Dr. Roberts wagged his snowy head. His white-thatched nostrils gleamed. "Well, I suppose it doesn't signify. I'm only old Harry Roberts, and I don't signify, though I *am* still on the Budget Committee. I guess I know a flapper when I see one, and I know a good bottle of Fundador when I see one, so pour me a glass, Silas Selby. Call me a Brandy Baptist if you like, what care I; I'm only old Harry Roberts and my years of labor don't signify. Pour me *two* glasses of good Spanish brandy, or I'll tell the Budget Committee about your stinking old head, and what will they say about *that*? —Ah. Hah ha. Mmmm. Tell you I know a flapper when I see one."

* * *

Edward Bagnell, Doctor of Philosophy, friend of Dave Branch, and holder of other distinctions greeted Vlad Smith and Jack Stewart in the Elephant Room of Sumner Public College's Museum of Ethnology. The Elephant Room contained a rather large and awful oil painting of the progress of some Hindu maharaja, the gift of a long-ago benefactor. The painting's cleaning was fiercely resisted on the grounds that it was best left obscured.

Bagnell waved them to a large leather sofa. "I daresay you'd like to know *why* it's Sumner *Public* College? *Every*body wants to. I am able to dispel the mystery. The founding fathers and the one founding mother put the word in to show that the college was a serf to neither church nor state. As some still *are.* How do you like the Elephant Room? It looks like the antechamber of a rather seedy club, but here the Department of Ethnology holds out by being part anthropology, part folklore, and part whatever. We claim to have pioneered the interdisciplinary study; haw. And *here* is where the ethnologists gather to drink embalming fluid, as wine is only allowed on campus for certain ceremonial occasions. How is Allbright doing?"

Stewart took the reply upon himself. "Old man gives the impression that he's mostly letting the kudzu grow over him, but he isn't really. And the boy makes cryptic statements such as 'Larraby's got one locked up.'" He repeated what he had told Vlad and concluded, "You have any idea what that means, Dr. Bagnell?"

Ed Bagnell shrugged. "Probably that Larraby, whoever he may be, has a report on the legend, and is keeping it locked up until he's ready to publish. Typical academic paranoia, eh Vlad?"

After answering no more than a grunt, Vlad slowly began to speak of his own and immediate problem. Of encountering by moonlight in the old uninhabited house, something so hideous, noisome, foul that he might have thought it was madness to think it was real. Only to find the sight so real as to drive his small daughter past terror and hysteria. "Do you understand why I'm trying to find out ..." he waved his hands helplessly, "... *what* the damned thing was? That, that *van*ished in an instant? One minute it was there, another minute *nothing* was there, as though, just as though it *had* come out of the wall. The police say 'Tramp'— it was no tramp! The only thing it resembled was that old legend, and that's why I'm here, Ed. In my file on the legend is a collection of items labeled *Bagnell's Notes.* I won't go so far as to say they are yellowed, but they are far from crisp. May I ask how *you* got interested in the legend of the Paper-Man, or whatever name you call it by?"

"I got interested when I read an unpublished paper on it, and remembered I'd long ago met a possible informant, and hadn't realized it. One day when I was a kid, I was walking in a strange part of town and I came to an old house, abandoned and all overgrown. I thought I'd go in and look around, when a creepy old man hobbled from out of nowhere, with torn old clothes, and just a few teeth grinding in stubbly jaws, and he smelled very funny. Later an old lumberjack said to me, as if reading my mind, 'Don't go in that old house, boy, a Boss in the Wall lives there. They're crazy people who think they're dead, and they wrap themselves in paper, and they rattle like snakes and bite like snakes, so don't go in there, boy.'"

Stewart paid the ultimate compliment. He sat straight up and said, "No shit?"

"But I decided that poor old man was just a bum or tramp, who staked out a place for himself and didn't want me inside. Years later I read the unpublished item, and all the elements fit, so naturally I became interested. I wrote a paper on the subject, and mine remains unpublished too. So there you are, gentlemen."

"What conclusions did you come to, for example, about the origins of the legend?" asked Vlad.

Bagnell shrugged. "It's like trying to trace down the origins of a fog. The fog exists and you can see it, but it always seems to begin somewhere else. Compare it to other American legends, that is, you can trace groundhog stories to badger stories, but then you trace them right back to groundhogs. Sometimes we folklorists take every possibility into consideration except the human longing for a good yarn, which sometimes means a good *scary* yarn." A twig snapped in the fireplace and Bagnell said, "If fireplaces were concealed inside walls, they might be called *snappers.* All the legends are attached to old houses, and old houses often creak. They attract drifters and outcasts of broken minds and unclean habits, who remind us of childhood terror-tales of ghosts and skeletons and god knows what. And so a legend evolves."

Vlad asked if Bagnell had anything new to show him. Bagnell suggested he might call Dave Branch, but Vlad reminded him that it was Branch who had sent him to Bagnell.

"Well," Bagnell said, "I don't know what to tell you, Vlad, I just don't know what to tell you."

Vlad did not move for a while, then he let himself sink back in the chair. Behind him hung a beautiful photograph, an enlargement in sepia of a group of Ainu at a long-ago American world's fair. They gazed through the camera as from some lost continent, too dignified to show their infinite bewilderment and their vast sense of doom.

After Vlad and Jack departed, Bagnell picked up the phone: "Dr. Bagnell returning Dr. Branch's call. Hello, Dave? Yes, I know you hadn't called; that's just a ploy, never fails—*sly*. Listen, one Vladimir Smith, Ph.D. He's tracking the Paper-Man legend. I just have one question: you *didn't* mention the Committee to him, did you? No, good, that's fine. Back to your learned discourses. Bye."

❋ ❋ ❋

"Rawheaded Bloody Bones" may be an undifferentiated spook, but

*it is certainly vividly different from the rather enigmatic "The Boss
in the Wall" which, to some informants, suggests an image of the
human mind trapped inside the skull, and which has been reported
from Mobile, Alabama, to Jacksonville, Florida, and on up the Atlantic
Coast for a few states more. "Rawheaded Bloody Bones" would
not remind you right away of the "Greasy-Man" of Corpus Christi,
Brownsville and Porta Isabella (all Texas). In all these places, however,
"Greasy-Man" is also known as "String-Fellow" or "The String-Fellow."
It's been conjectured that the latter name may come from the jerky,
puppet-like walk attributed to the phenomenon. In New Orleans, of
course, where every superstition flourishes, most of these names may
be found, plus, as might be expected, the zomby-zumbi-jumbie-duppy
group of names (see Limekiller): with the important difference that no
"Paper-Man" etc. has ever been alleged "held to service or labor." In
other words, Zomby may have been at one time a slave, but Paper-Man
was not.*
—*Bagnell's Notes*

* * *

Bagnell had arranged for Vlad and Jack to stay in a college
guesthouse where Bagnell himself had recently stayed while his
house was being painted. In the drawer of a nightstand Vlad
found a sheaf of forgotten papers, labeled *Duplicate of Dr. Bagnell's
Committee Report.* Vlad felt a twinge of scruple. Should he read it?
But what has been duplicated can hardly be personal. So ...

"Mr. Ernest Anderson is a trapper in a nearby state.

He and his family moved into a structure known locally as 'the
Old Linsey Mill.' The exterior is brick, but the inside is built of
more eclectic materials. The main mill building has been closed
for years, and the family lives in part of it. From the start of
their residence there, it seems there were odd noises and odd
smells, and one of the children claimed to have seen something.
Mr. Anderson, being a trapper, set a number of traps. On the night
of the given date, a loud noise was heard from the second floor,

described as the rattling and thrashing of a creature caught in a trap. Mr. Anderson and other male relatives left the living quarters to rush upstairs, but then they heard loud screams and ran back to the living quarters, because one of the children was having some sort of fit."

Here Vlad's blood ran cold as he continued reading …

"Mr. Anderson drove the child to the West County Medical Center, and it wasn't until much later that he was able to check the upstairs trap. It had been sprung, and inside the trap was a badly crushed, but easily identifiable human foot that seemed to be in a mummified condition. There was no sign of blood, and there was an immensely strong and fetid odor. I asked Mr. Anderson if the force of the trap being sprung could have severed the foot from the ankle. He answered, and remember that he has long been a trapper; he said that the foot had been gnawed off."

Attached to the pages was an envelope, and inside the envelope was a horrible close-up photograph. Of the foot. Vlad let the pages flutter away. He tried to swallow, but found that he could not. After a while he got up and went for a glass of water.

"You all right, Vlad?" asked Jack from the adjoining room.

"No, I am not."

"Want to tell me about it?"

"No, I don't." Vlad gave him the papers. Jack read them and looked up with an expression part puzzled, part unhappy. Vlad handed him the envelope. Jack looked at the photograph, then looked at Vlad with horrified eyes. "Jesus," he said.

Vlad said, "What the hell? Is this a loop? Am I a prisoner in a Moebius strip, or is it all a bad dream?"

Jack Stewart said, "No, it's not a bad dream. I'm sorry, I wish it were. I still don't know what it means, but it's not what we thought it meant—what we were told it meant. We're in another country from now on. A country with strange inhabitants and unknown boundaries."

IV
Bagnell's Quest

Bagnell was walking, on his way to see Larraby again.
Who first developed the notion of The Phenomenon of
the One-Legged Man in the Blue Baseball Cap? Bagnell did
not know, but he knew the phenomenon well enough. You never
saw such a person in your life, the story went, and the first day
you see him, you see two more. Not merely two, mind you, but two
more. Walking past the row of old stores which had, almost too
late, been saved from destruction by a committee of concerned
citizens—concerned, and prosperous—called Rowan Row, simply
because it was on Rowan Street; walking along on the other side of
the street, Bagnell looked up. He looked up with a jerk of his head;
he had not intended to stop, for he had walked slowly past the old
buildings earlier, had looked in the shop windows, seen nothing
he wanted to examine closely; he looked up now with a jerk of his
head. Had he seen, could he have seen a sign reading *Paper-Man*?
He had not. Not quite.

The shop buildings were all of brick and one story high, and
dated from the 1830s. Some attempt had been made to preserve
or restore the period flavor: where the tobacco store had been
was a tobacco store now, and outside it was a wooden Indian.
Apothecary's had a row of very attractive apothecary's jars on
display, plus antique equipment in a glass case, and as for the rest,
offered exactly what was sold in any other drugstore.

PasTime Paper Antiques, the sign read; which Bagnell had seen out of the corner of his ever-ready-to-deceive-you eyes. It had not caught his attention at first because it was, actually, above eye-level on its own side of the street. He stared a moment. He crossed the street. In the window were such things as well-weathered marriage documents illuminated in color in the Pennsylvania Dutch *fraktur* style, with flowering trees never seen even in botanical gardens, on the boughs of which were *distelfinks*, birds unknown to ornithology. There were a pair of U.S. Navy certificates identifying Chauncey Casey as *Caulker* and Clarence Casey as *Sailmaker*, dated in the 1890s. There were a few posters in extravagant tints, and a small sedate notice, *more inside*. Bagnell noticed a selection of lacy valentines.

Bagnell noticed the Paper-Man in the very front part of the window.

An old-fashioned bell bobbed and dipped and rang as Bagnell swung the door widely open. An informally, neatly-dressed gentleman in perhaps his early forties appeared from behind an oriental screen. "If there were a time-travel machine," the man said, quizzing his eyebrows, "I'd go back and murder whoever it was who cut something out of this copy of *Godey's Ladies' Book*, October 1842. Just imagine. Does this interest you? Yours for a dollar." He thrust it forward, but Bagnell did not thrust a dollar at him.

"I'd like to see one of the daguerreotypes in the window," Bagnell said. He realized that he was speaking very fast. He realized that he was breathing very fast. "The second one from the right."

"Certainly. Please help yourself," the man gestured to two bowls on a little table, and went forward to the window. With great control, Bagnell did not go with him, did not even turn to watch him. He examined the bowls. One contained small candies; the other was full of business cards reading:

PasTime Paper Antiques
Number 7, Rowan Row
Mr. Sydney, Proprietor

Mr. Sydney, Proprietor, returned. He held in his hand what looked like a tiny book, and handed it to Bagnell, who at once unclasped the tiny hook and re-opened it: it was the right one. It was the likeness of a young man in uniform, in no way remarkable, one might see him or his mates today drinking canned beer and watching television anywhere in town. Anywhere in the United States. "That is real leather and real brass, the casing, I mean, hardly to be found anymore anywhere; and the same goes for the satin facing the picture."

Bagnell asked the price, and Mr. Sydney slipped behind the screen and returned with a loose-leaf notebook which he now consulted. "Ah, yes. The collection of six daguerreotypes, I must tell you that they are actually ambrotypes, a slightly later process, but I follow your own usage which is my own as well; the collection of six daguerreotypes are for sale at $1,000, plus, alas, state sales tax of 3.7 percent. Sell only the single one? Oh, I am *afraid* not. They are after all a collection, and I couldn't sell just one. Not for less than $200, that is. And no, we don't take credit cards or out-of-state checks. Sorry. These are after all collectors' items, and a *very* good investment." He proceeded to tell Bagnell about one such which had appreciated even as it sat in the window; adding, "Though if these are still here when the weather gets hotter, of course I will bring them inside because I am afraid of them fading."

* * *

Curator Luke Larraby gave a grunt of surprise at seeing Bagnell again so soon, but he was not uncivil, and listened to him without interruption. He said, "Calm down, we're not used to excitement here, in fact haven't had any since the Yankee army passed through town, thank the Lord they didn't even stop to burn it. Excitement, yes. I don't feel I can discount the possibility that you are still in a state of excitement—even shock. It is a shocking sight, that photograph of mine—and those things I showed you. So ... Oh of course I'll go stroll by and take a look at the one you say is in ... where? Rowan Row. Oh." He looked at the card Bagnell gave him.

"It would be one of the most remarkable coincidences if, actually, they were—Ho. Mr. Sydney, yes. Know him. Done business with him, business, you get the point? Sydney is not running a junkyard. Now settle down. Rome wasn't built in a day. *Quit that fidgeting.*"

Bagnell extended his stay at his motel, drove slowly back to the old Carolina Coast Museum, went up the blue slate steps, scooped and hollowed by the passing feet of a century. Larraby was there, and beckoned him in from inside his private office. "Aw right. Saw—it. What? *Course* it's the same face! Out*ra*geous coincidence! Against all known laws of probability. However. We must have a copy of Sydney's ambro and work from there. No other choice. And it's up to you to get him to let you make that copy. They're not photographic negatives, you know that, of course. We'll have to photograph it and produce our own negative. Enlarge it. Well— enlarge them *both.* Go over them with magnifying lens and fine-tooth comb. Have you got $200 cash on you, by the way? Ha. *Thought* not."

Bagnell found himself breathing rapidly again. "Look here, Luke"—a silvery-tufted eyebrow shot up, but Larraby listened —"this is absolutely the first time it's been even possible to think of its being even possible to provide any element of pre-history of a Paper-Man, and you can't let it go by and risk losing it forever."

Larraby, still calm in his naturally cool old-fashioned office, with sepia-tinted framed photographs of his predecessors on its walls; Larraby, still calm, said it was Bagnell's fault for showing enthusiasm. "However. I understand your emotion. Still, why he wants $200, $200 for a daguerreotype of a nobody, for that price you ought to get one of Lola Montez naked—and I have not got that $200 in my budget."

Bagnell gnawed his neat mustache. "Well, how much have you got that you can spend to borrow the picture, just borrow it and have it copied? I mean, you absorb the copying costs, and I'm sure I can manage a pro rata share of it—how much?"

The old curator sighed and canted his head and looked at his wall calendar. "Oh ... $50? *Tops.*"

* * *

Mr. Sydney was cautious. Mr. Sydney smelled something.

Bagnell offered to have it cleaned for him. "No charge."

"*Cleaned*? It's as clean as a whistle! Look at it. Beautiful condition. What—"

"Okay. I'll come clean with you."

"Now we're talking."

"The Carolina Coast Museum—"

"The Carolina Coast Mu—Oh, Lord, *they* don't have a *but*ton! Nothing doing. Oh, well, what's your offer?"

"An offer of $50 just to—"

Mr. Sydney's shock was not assumed. "Fifty *do*llars! *No* no. Out of the—"

"—just to borrow it for one week for purposes of comparison with another picture."

This was unexpected. Mr. Sydney seemed genuinely uncertain. "And what do I do if someone comes in off the Row and asks, 'Where's the old snapshot of the boy in uniform, used to be in between Baby Phoebe and Grampa Jukes?'"

"You say, 'It's being cleaned. Would you like to put down a deposit? It will be cleaned for you. Free.'"

It was immediately clear that Mr. Sydney liked this image. He nodded. His mouth moved, evidently silently repeating the words. "You have a suggestion there. Not bad. Very well. I feel able to do it for you and the museum, but for $75. Impossible for less: risk factor."

Slowly, Bagnell emptied his pockets. There was the fairly crisp $50. And, also, there was a limp $20, and two dim ones, and 50 cents. His sigh was quite immediate. So was Mr. Sydney's reaction. "Oh, very well, the Firm will settle for $70, and will cover state tax. The Firm is not hard-hearted. Keep the two-fifty for lunch. The Museum will probably offer you possum *a la taxidermy.* Oh, and I shall require you to show some ID and to sign a little piece of paper, and then shall I gift wrap it for you? No? But remember now: *Not more than one week.*"

＊　＊　＊

"Company in the parlor," Curator Larraby said, briskly.

Bagnell blinked. "An odd phrase to come from a self-admitted church-member."

Company, in the small lecture-room (doors locked), consisted of Hughes of the Southeastern Interstate Criminology Institute (commonly called the Crim Lab), and Dr. Preston Budworth of every hospital in town. "My colleagues insist that the best specialty is dermatology. They say, 'The patients never die and they never get cured; they just keep coming back.' And I say, 'True, but plastic surgeons make more. Oh boy yes. Of course, we work hard for it, oh it's hell on the feet.'"

He said no more for the moment, the lights having then been turned off; then he said, "Jesus *Christ!*"—the slide of the Paper-Man's head having briefly flashed on the screen. "Course I've seen worse," said Dr. Budworth. "Oh lots worse. But seen nothing the same. What in salvation *is* it?" The copy of the ambrotype next appeared. "Soldier boy, hey?" It remained a while, then the severed head, with its cold, sly sneer, came back to grimace at them. Dr. Budworth cleared his throat and said, "Looks as though he'd been shot dead at Gettysburg and had his picture taken at Appomattox."

In a voice slow and heavy, Larraby said, "Perhaps you're right."

There was a silence then, broken by Hughes asking, "Is this your question, Curator? 'Are these two pictures of the same man?' Is that it?" Larraby said, Yes, that was it. Was asked to show both slides side by side. Did so. Hughes then said he thought they might well be. "For example, that drooping—Oh, excuse me, Dr. Budworth." But Budworth told him to go on. "—that drooping eyelid. And then you observe the crease in the earlobe. Can you see that really very slight scar on the cheekbone, on the opposite side from the drooping eyelid? And, ah, of course in the, I assume, postmortem photo, some of the teeth are exposed, and you see that the left canine is crooked and protrudes. Of course in the one in uniform, he has his mouth closed, but there is still a slight protrusion just over where that canine would be.

"Now, these are technical observations, though not very technical, and of course my simple guess would have been anyway that it is the same person, some years apart, though I wouldn't offhand guess how many. Not more than ten, I'd say. Maybe even five, or a bit less, since … war being war, you know …"

The "postmortem" photo, a perfectly correct description, certainly, had been cropped in the copying process, and it was not evident that the head was separate from the torso. If Hughes suspected anything, Hughes was not saying. To Bagnell, trying to put aside what he knew, merely the difference in the photographic techniques, more than a century apart, was obvious.

Preston Budworth's comments were more technical, but he came to the same conclusion. "Of course I would want to make measurements and enlarge the pictures even more, on as close to even-scale as possible, before I'd sign my name to anything, not that I'm going to, anyway. Historical detective work is lots of fun, of course, and nobody waiting to sue you for malpractice. Well. I wouldn't want to ask where you got that ghouly-looking one from."

Promptly, Hughes said, "*I* would. I *will*. *Where?*"

But they did not tell him. Not yet.

* * *

Military historians identified uniform coat and badges as those of the 23rd Patriot Rifles. Phone calls in all directions finally produced Charles O'Neill Sturtevant, Col., USA (Ret.), who had an enormous collection of Civil War photographs. And—

"Mind you, young man, it's a *loan*. Your balls are in bond for it."

"Yes, Colonel, of course, any time you like, sir," babbled Bagnell, scarcely knowing what he was saying.

On that red-letter day, against what awesome odds, Ed Bagnell found what he was hoping for: printed off a cracked wet-plate, though only slightly cracked, the likenesses of three young men, frozen stolid, hands on knees; and on the back the signatures —two florid and scrawly/scrolly, one awkward and cramped— Corporal W.M. Ewing. Private Elwen Michaels. Private Ephraim Mackilwhit.

Now for the first time, there was a *name*.

* * *

The 23rd Patriot Rifles had been enlisted in Gainsboro, as far to the South as it was perhaps possible for a Northern town to be, and there Bagnell went as fast as was consistent with speed laws, and energy consistent with small packets of crackers-and-cheese sold in gas stations. In the Gainsboro phone book he pushed a restless finger down the columns in search of people named Mackilwhit.

He found not one.

That is, the current one contained not one. At the public library, in the reference room: "Out of date telephone directories? Nooo. We don't keep them."

"Oh ..." Sinking voice, sinking feeling.

"But I'll tell you who *does*. Mr. Rodeheaver does. I'll write down the address for you."

Homer would have felt at home in the old room where Mr. Rodeheaver worked. Bagnell felt that if he had wanted the directory for Fusby-le-Mud, 1901, it would have been there. Mr. Rodeheaver perhaps collected them, perhaps compiled mailing lists, or traced missing heirs. Bagnell didn't care. Mr. Rodeheaver was getting on in years and he listened patiently; then he asked, "What's it worth to you?"

"Worth—?"

"Is it worth five dollars?"

Mr. Rodeheaver began to pull down old phone books and pile

them on his dusty desk; beckoned Bagnell to come look. Waited while he did. Ceasing three years before, but as far back from then, farther back than Bagnell cared to go, a Mrs. Lambert Mackilwhit had lived at 269 Longfellow Avenue. Bagnell copied the address, handed the man a crumpled five dollar bill.

"Well, there's lunch," said Mr. Rodeheaver.

Did she still live there? Had she died three years ago? Had she just given up her phone, there being too few left alive to call her? Or, perhaps, there had been some difficulty about a bill, and she had let her listing lapse, and had a phone installed in the name of a neighbor, friend, or ... well, probably not. But. Hurt to try? Might find a lead. Leads had been found, one after another.

Two-sixty-nine was in rather better shape than the other houses, which had all once been neat and bright ... long ago ... and Mrs. Mackilwhit lived in a little room on the top floor, whither he was directed by a series of ageless women in cotton housedresses, of whom each seemed to have three children and one in utero. But Mrs. Mackilwhit was not ageless. Mrs. Mackilwhit was very aged indeed, and her skin hung in heavy flaps.

Did she know of an Ephraim Mackilwhit, who had served in the Civil War? A silence. The room smelled, rather, but of nothing worse than old people's flesh and of cabbage, and perhaps it was only the neighbors' cabbage. The room contained what was left of her life as it had drawn in upon itself, decade after decade; there was hardly room enough to move, although no doubt the woman who lived there had moved enough. She sat in her chair and she did not move now, and she stared at nothing which other people could see.

Silence. Then—"He disappeared," she said at last. "Lambert's, my husband's aunts, used to speak of him. He was the black sheep of the family. He went away and he never came back. Yes. He disappeared."

Bagnell had brought another picture along, of another group of soldiers, as a sort of control, and now he put both in her hands. "Might you recognize a family resemblance?"

She pushed one away after a glance, but the other one she looked at long and long. "A family resemblance. Yes. The one at the end. On the right. He has Lambert's look. Yes. He has Lambert's look." And, very silently, her slow tears rained along the ruined landscape of her face.

A family resemblance. *Is not Ephraim a beloved child*? And what had he come to? A thing in three boxes: shriveled, withered, broken, and foul. But now at last, thank God forever dead.

*   *   *

Bagnell to Larraby: "Where was Ephraim Mackilwhit ... that is, where was the Paper-Man found? Come clean."

"Basement storeroom, in an old private girls' school in Gainsboro, couple years ago. Mustee was picking up a little extra money there as a weekend relief watchman," said Larraby.

Thither went Dr. Claire Zimmerman, at Bagnell's request, to interview the headmistress, Mrs. Sidwell:

"Yes, this *is* one of the oldest houses in town. It is well-preserved, and consequently required no major restorations. It has made an excellent private school building." Mrs. Sidwell stopped and thought. "Do I recall anything *odd* happening a couple of years ago? Well, there was a ... I suppose the word I have to use is *prank*. It's difficult to say when a prank gets out of hand and becomes ... something more. Dr. Rose Bennett asked me into her Advanced English class during a morning break. She said there was something on the blackboard she didn't like. Of course I expected what we used to call a naughty word. *Are* there anymore naughty words? I haven't quite grown used to hearing sweet girls talking like sailors. Well, no, it wasn't a naughty word. The words *Nothing but Death* were written on the blackboard, and the writing was odd ... somehow *wrong*. The next day the same words were written on a blackboard in room A-6, and the following morning, there it was again. Security and maintenance promised to keep a close watch on room A-6, and the next day the words *Nothing but Death* appeared in room C-12! When that happened, *every*body began to get nervous. Well, we photographed the words, sponged all the blackboards, and read the riot act to security and maintenance, but still it appeared. Of course you'd like to see it ..." Mrs. Sidwell rummaged in a drawer and handed an enlarged photograph to Claire, who studied it intently.

"Then Rose Bennett remembered that those were Jane Austen's dying words. But the handwriting bore no resemblance to samples of Jane Austen's, and we weren't even teaching Jane Austen that year. So our school was being haunted by a spectre with a good knowledge of early 19th century English literature. But who?"

"Judging from the cramped and wavering writing, it must have been somebody very sick, or very tired," said Claire.

"Oh my, I don't like the sound of that, though you're probably right. I must say, the whole thing gave me the creeps. Do you think somebody very *old* wrote it? The writing looks so weak and old fashioned. But why would an old person come creeping in like that? I asked Rose Bennett what the class had been discussing, the day before the words appeared. She remembered that she had asked them, 'If you could be granted only one wish, what would you wish for?' The next morning, the words began to appear: *Nothing but death*. Then just as suddenly, it stopped."

Claire examined the photograph closely. "What's that down at the bottom of the blackboard? It looks like the letters 'E.M.' in the same writing."

"Oh yes, sometimes that appeared too. But nobody knew what it meant," said Mrs. Sidwell. And then the bell rang and she had to go.

✻ ✻ ✻

Vlad Smith and Jack Stewart were bedded down in an old-fashioned Tourist Guesthouse for the night. It was owned by Mrs. Warrington, who looked like a gentlewoman in reduced circumstances. A bottle and glasses stood on the table next to a small pile of rather unprofessional-looking printed matter.

Jack tugged a comb through his tangled molasses curls and

picked one up. "Nice old guy who gave us these," he said. "Mr. Pabrocky. All these years he's been sending you these things and then all of a sudden you turn up on his doorstep. *The News Bulletin of the Atlantic Folk Lore*, two words and no hyphen, very dubious usage, *Club*," he read. "Volume XV, number 11, to be precise. *WHO'S BOSS IN YOUR WALL? Cute, hey?" There is a story told particularly in the southeastern and south central states of a spook or specter or bogle or hant who inhabitants houses and other older, usually, buildings. He is musty and gant and lives in the walls and floors and empty rooms and is seldom seen. The description is that he is skeletal but unlike other such myths he is depicted as wearing old clothes and is afraid of cats and fires. Perhaps because he is all dried up? It is quite a task to look this subject up in indexes and bibliographies, for one thing because it has so many names and for another so little seems to have been published. So we urge our members to make inquiries wherever they happen to be. Perhaps our little amateur News Bulletin may provide some information which the learned quarterlies have not. This folk tale figure is called 'Paper-Man' because he lives behind the wall paper which used to be on every wall but now no longer owing to the high cost and labor and also, we assume, because of a prejudice that 'Bugs' breed there. This creature issues a noise which is variously described as clicking or clattering or even rustling. Hence the various names of 'Rustler' or 'Clicker' as well as 'the Boss in the Wall.' Another name is 'House-Devil' and Mary Mae Subchak reports she has heard it referred to as 'the Devil in the Wall.'"*

Stewart next applied his lips to a glass, then said, "Well, I would give this a ... a B-minus. You, Dr. Smith? Trouble with amateurs, they are always reinventing the wheel."

"*MORE ON PAPER-MAN NAMES (CONT.)*" Jack read. "*We find that the so-called 'Minorcan' descended people of St. Augustine, Fla., employ the name or term 'Clicky Dicky.' Alas for our hopes that we might find some such Spanish survival variants. Crossing the peninsula to Pensacola, we note that 'Clicky Dicky' has become 'Tricky Dicky,' a term extending as far south on that coast as Tampa. We were unable to find this legend at all in St. Petersburg, Fla., an absence tentatively attributed to the Northern-Origin of So Many Of The*

People in the 'Winter Capital.' Mr. Pabrocky has suggested, with the well-known twinkle in his eye, that it is remarkable nonetheless that neither 'Clicker' nor 'Clicky Dicky' is to be found where there are so many Senior Citizens (of whom he is one!), considering how many of them have the medically well-known condition, 'a clicking knee-cap'! Humor apart, this does raise the QUESTION, if the 'clicking' attributed to the spectre comes from the sound of teeth as had generally been believed or to some other source. Hmmm." Jack put the *News Bulletin* down.

Vlad sighed wearily. "Is there any more brandy in the bottle?"

There was no more brandy in the bottle. They argued back and forth about opening another bottle. Each took both sides. Then they opened another bottle.

"Should we read more mind-improving books now?" asked Jack.

Vlad said he'd rather *write* a mind-improving book called, *"The Myth of the Paper-Man Examined and Refuted.* Even that title shows how far I've come in my thinking. A month ago I'd no more have needed to refute it than I would have refuted Dracula or Frankenstein. Household words; everybody knows about them, but nobody *believes* in them, or cowers in *fear* of them."

Jack slipped a cassette of Buxtehude's *Misa Brevis* into his lil' ole cassette player. His movements made goofy shadows on the wall. "That nice?" he asked.

"More than nice, it's ravishing," said Vlad sleepily. "When it's over, play it again, Sam."

Perhaps Sam had played it again, but now it was not playing. A shadow was playing on the floor, which *goofy* would not describe. It looked like the shadow of an enormous four-legged spider gliding upside down across the floor. Whatever it was looked horrible. Dear god, would he forever be seeing horrid and impossible things?

Jack was sitting up in his bed with his face gone ghastly. Then he leaped out of his bed and out of their room, and went roaring and running down the hallway. "Where did it go? Did you *see* it, Vlad? It ran along the *ceiling!*" Jack dragged a table and chair into the hallway and started to climb on it.

Mrs. Warrington appeared, with her hair in a gray-streaked braid, and a man's bathrobe over her nightgown. She stretched out her hands and called, "Mr. Stewart! You must stop this *now!*"

"Miz Warrington! Where did it go? Where did it come from? What *lives* in this hallway?"

Many expressions passed rapidly over her worn face, but now they settled into one expression: a gentlewoman in reduced circumstances. "Mr. Stewart," she said in a quick but firm and level voice, "I am very sorry that you had a bad dream, but I will not be shouted at in my own house, and I refuse to hold a conversation with a strange man in his underwear. Please take the table and chair *back*, sir!"

"No I *won't*, Miz Warrington, not yet. Please excuse me ma'am," said Jack, as he climbed onto the table and chair, and began to examine the imperfect surface of the ceiling.

Mrs. Warrington was actually wringing her hands. "What is he *doing*? Can't you make him stop, Professor Smith? You have terrified me with those awful yells, and now *this*! What is it?"

Jack said in doleful tones, "It didn't rattle or click, but I know what it is, ma'am, and I reckon you know too."

The woman's face seemed to collapse in upon itself, and she tottered and leaned against the wall, for just a moment, then sprang away as though it were red-hot.

Her voice was now trembling but fierce. "This guesthouse is all I have to live on. I don't know who you are, but I want you to get out right *now*. I don't want your money, please *go!*"

They went as soon as they could dress and pack. Without discussion they left money on the table. Then they got into the car and drove in silence, with Vlad behind the wheel. His sallow face was weary, and his blue-gray eyes were troubled and gray.

"What did you see?" Vlad finally asked.

"I woke up and saw this *thing* scuttling across the ceiling. Something like a man, but horribly bony and filthy, and utterly nasty in some way I can't describe. You?"

"I just saw the shadow," said Vlad. "I never heard of one on the ceiling."

"It was clinging by its long nails to the tiny gaps in the plaster, and the flaps of torn clothing swayed, and that vile body swayed too. I don't know where it came from, or where it went to. There's no window or hatchway, only a little ventilation slit that maybe a rat could get through, but not a *man*."

Eventually they stopped at the brightest and newest motel they could find, with walls too thin for even a roach to hide.

* * *

Mr. Pabrocky's *News Bulletin* led Vlad and Jack to a privately endowed art museum. They were repeating a list of names to the "museum lady," and the list had begun to seem very tiresome and, indeed, loathsome. "... or the Boss in the Wall ...?" Vlad finished the list, and a look of great surprise came over her face.

She said, "Of *course*. Hobson's Ghost. You know that all institutions have their skeletons in the closet. That one is ours. Long ago we bought what is known as a 'primitive' portrait, meaning it was painted by a self-taught, itinerant artist. It showed a woman sitting in a room. Evidently something was painted into the picture which wasn't apparent. Something was painted over, and then the over-paint sloughed off. It rose to the surface like a ghost, and it was ghost-like, and quite famous for a while. But finally we had to take the picture off exhibition because parents complained that it scared their children—and it probably scared *them*. On the old acquisition slip is written *Hobson.* We aren't sure if that's the subject or the artist, and faintly penciled in is *Boss in the Wall.* Whatever *that* means. Would you like to see it?"

Primitive it certainly was. A late middle-aged woman sat stiffly in a chair in an old-fashioned room. Her skirt was long and black, her shawl was white, and her face was stiff. Above her was something gray and ghastly that seemed to ooze from a panel in the wall. It looked like the bleached carapace of a long-dead spider, with bared teeth, and skeletal hands with clawing nails. Its expression was both fearful and malignant. *Hobson's Ghost.*

"Oh god, yes," said Vlad in a sick, weak voice. "That's it ... a Boss in the Wall. Do you know any more about it?"

"Well, there is an old story about a Henry and Hannah Hobson, who were settlers over in Blainesville. He was a widower, she a widow. He wanted to move west to live with his children. She wanted to move east to live with *her* children. Folks didn't divorce or separate in those days, so they quarreled day and night. Then either he got sick and she let him die without calling a doctor, or she slowly poisoned his food. Anyway, his last words were that he'd never leave the house alive—and neither would she. And after he died, she never *did* leave. She packed more than once, but never left. Then old Hobson began to haunt her. One time or another, that wretched woman lived in every room of the house. No use. He'd find her, so in the end she hanged herself. There's even an old *song* about it," The museum lady began to sing in a wavering voice:
"How the night winds howl, for death seems near to me.
Beware, Mr. Hobson, do not drink that tea!
I fear my time is fleeting, and death comes in a rush.
Beware, Mr. Hobson, do not sup that mush!
I fear my bad wife Hannah, and I fear my time has come.
Beware, Mr. Hobson, do not drink that rum!
So stand back good Christian people, and do not heed her calls.
For to haunt my bad wife Hannah, I slink slowly through the walls!"

※ ※ ※

Now Vlad and Jack were talking to Henry Wabershaw. "I'm named for my grandfather's old Russian friend, Vladimir, for Smithville is full of Edgars, but how many *Vlad* Smiths are there?" said Vlad.

If, inside of Wabershaw's great fat man's body there was a thin man screaming to get out, the screaming was inaudible to either Vlad or Jack. "You fellows from The Committee?" asked Wabershaw, in a small voice almost stifled by his immense flesh.

"The committee?" asked Vlad. "That makes as much sense as

'Larraby's got one.'"

Perhaps Wabershaw understood the nuances of the remark and perhaps he did not. What he said was, "So you know about Larraby, hmm?" He nodded the small face set inside the very large one, and gave them an odd look. After a moment he sighed and said, "I'm sorry I can't ask you boys to have a bite to eat, but there's not a bite in the house." He gazed at them as if he had given a sign and were waiting for a countersign.

Vlad and Jack had been warned that the way to Wabershaw's heart and head was through his stomach, for he was surely eating himself to death. So they were prepared. Stewart now said, "As to that, Mr. Wabershaw, as we hadn't yet had our dinner, we took the liberty of bringing a little something along, and wondered if you'd have some with us." He lifted the large paper sacks onto the table.

"Why, *fried* chicken! I always say that fried chicken is the friend of man. And how I love potato salad! *Three* kinds of bread, *real* butter, French mustard, and look at these tempting cold cuts! Oh, I am very fond of raspberry soda. And what might be in this other bag? *Chinese* food! Is there anything nicer than Chinese food?" Then he peeped into a cardboard box and exclaimed with almost erotic glee, "What a *lovely* cake!" Pieces of fried chicken were already on the way to his turtle-like mouth when he paused and said, "*You* boys aren't from The Committee. Catch any of them giving anything—they just *take*! Bagnell, Calloway, Zimmerman, Elbaum, Branch, and the rest of that bunch. They want it *all* for themselves."

"*Branch*!" cried Vlad.

By and by the galloping consumption of food slowed down to a mere nibbling. Wabershaw surveyed the wreckage on the table with elephantine calm and said, "Happiest day in my life."

"Which day was that?" asked Vlad.

"When I first realized that the Boss in the Wall was *real*! Why? Because on that day I knew for sure that I was not going crazy."

"I can appreciate that," said Vlad with heartfelt sincerity.

"When you've been hearing things you can't see, and seeing things you can't believe, why, a fear builds up inside you and your life sort of slumps sideways into a different universe. I tried staying away from home, sleeping in the office and sleeping in hotels. I tried getting drunk and staying drunk, and I lost my good job as State Historian. I was hospitalized twice for nervous breakdowns, and in the hospital I began to put on flesh. Then one day I realized I was not crazy, so I came home. And I found a man with trained ferrets, and we sent those ferrets into the walls. Then we heard a terrible thrashing sound in the storeroom, and by the time we got there it was dead—but it had bit some of the ferrets to pieces. The man was pretty mad, and made me pay plenty for the loss of his critters. But I rejoiced, for just the sight and smell of that House-Devil proved I wasn't crazy. I burned it in the fireplace, for it was very dry. And now I keep openings in the walls for my cats, who can git to any part of this house, and who serve to give warning if needed. You can feel *safe* here, professors. This house has been purged. This house is pure."

Vlad recalled Pappa John's words to Uncle Mose. *"Git you a cat."*

Then Wabershaw placed his vasty paw over Vlad's very ordinary hand, in a reassuring way that persuaded Vlad that once upon a time, before he became an eccentric though harmless monster, Henry Wabershaw must have been a very nice fellow. He said, "So now I stay home, for I no longer fear for my sanity. And I don't drink any more—I just eat."

Vlad said, "You have come face to face with the same thing which persuaded us that this myth is no myth—namely, we have also seen the creatures. Now the question is how did they come to exist? For if we know what started them, maybe we'll know how to stop them."

Wabershaw shifted his great weight in his reinforced chair, reached in a drawer and handed Vlad a manila envelope. "Seen anything like this?" he asked, as Vlad removed a sheaf of papers labeled *First Draft of the Interim Committee Report.*

Vlad made a sound of surprise, for the papers were in the same format as those Bagnell had left behind in the nightstand of the Sumner College guesthouse. He began to read:

"... *They are commonly known as Rattlers or Rustlers but, in places*

as far apart as San Francisco and St. Louis, the favorite term is
Clickers. In certain border states, the obscure Hyett is found, which
may be related to Rawheaded Bloody Bones. In Biloxi, the favored
terms are Boss-Devil, or Devil in the Wall. Dr. Allan Lee Murrow, the
great Southern folklorist says this may be an extension of the zomby
legends, or that the zomby may have its origins here. Dr. Robert
Allbright notes the Yazoo Delta fable that Hyetts died of yellow fever
or plague, and eat human flesh.

"Hamling Calloway M.D. raises the question of whether there might
be an unidentified retrovirus or microorganism, somehow associated
with the great plagues (perhaps as a 'fellow traveler'), which might in
some way cause the phenomena that lie at the bottom of these tales.
Something which resembles life; some unrecognized viral wasting
syndrome or plague which causes pseudo-life. And if so, is this plague
still active—now?"

Vlad let the papers drop on the still-littered table, sighed and
rubbed his eyes. "What do *you* think?" he asked Wabershaw.

"Professors, as near as I am confident, there is a disease, never
diagnosed, which simulates death—and which then simulates
life. And which still, from time to time, simulates it *now*. From
the time when their normal body processes sink below a certain
point, those old Paper-Men are neither alive as we know it, nor
dead as we know it. They lie motionless behind countless walls,
not crumbling to dust, until something *disturbs* them, and then
they go clickin' and clattering, and rustlin' and rattling—until
their clock runs down again. Then they go back inside the walls
until something winds them up again. I have often wondered how
many of those poor old derelicts we see nodding and mumbling in
doorways of old buildings, are in fact suffering from Paper-Man's
disease. They wrap themselves in rags and newspapers to stay
warm, and crawl into a niche in some wall. They keep themselves
'alive' with an occasional rat, for rats are known to run along
walls, and they sink into a hibernating state until something
wakes them—then they attack. I knew all this before those fancy
committee fellows did. I tried to tell them, but they wouldn't
listen, *they* knew better. Well, hell with'm. Young Professor

Stewart, there's a gallon of sweet melk in the icebox, if you'd be so kind to bring it out."

V
The Committee

Gertrude (Mrs. Harry Brown) Roberts had finally, after years of trying everything in the pharmacopoeia, found something which would put her to sleep and keep her to sleep. Ten minutes after she had taken it—an interval long enough to read her nightly number of lines from the Bible and to say her prayers (she now left the Catholics and Episcopalians for last, as she drifted into slumber)—her toothless mouth would open in her bony face and she would begin to snore. This, as it usually woke him up, was her old husband's signal that he was once again a free man for the night.

"So, Gertrude Sayer," he hissed at the unresponsive body on the far side of the bed; "taking more than a thimbleful of brandy is *wrong*, is it? But doping your soul into subconsciousness with that chemical counterfeit of poppy and mandragore is all right, is it? Stuff! Poppycock! But just like a Sayer!"

Old Harry Roberts got out of bed; the night air being just a bit chill, he put on his second-best frock coat (the one he saved for commencements and inaugurations, saving the very best one for Board meetings) over his nightshirt, and shuffled along the street in his carpet slippers. There were no passers-by and had there been, few would have given him a second glance and had any done so it would have been a glance of approval. New England still dearly cherished its eccentrics … had any identified him as one.

H. Brown Roberts was soon at a certain side door to the

General Museum of the Province of Rhode Island and Providence Plantations, of which he was still Librarian Emeritus and a member of the Budget Committee. He let himself in with his keys. A moment later he was once again deep into the immense annals of the Underground Railroad, on which he had long planned a series of books, and thus he stayed. From time to frequent time he muttered to himself about the Fugitive Slave Act and the Free Soil Whigs, and his great grandmother Brown and his great grandfather Roberts, both of whom were conductors on the Underground Railroad; when glancing up he observed one of the passengers.

"Oh, my poor fellow!" H.B.R. exclaimed, rising to his feet. "Are you one of the stowaways aboard the cotton-boat from Charleston? Never do fear, we shall see you safe to Canada ... but perhaps you are hungry, did they give you some hot victuals in the kitchen? What? Not? Well just you come with me." The hallway seemed a trifle strange to him, as he padded along it, followed by the silent figure. Presently they entered another room, which he did not precisely recognize as either a part of the old Roberts or of the old Brown house ... though to be sure, some of the furnishings ... It was not the kitchen, whatever it was, although ... "Ha! There is the porcelain ginger-jar which Merchant Houqua of the Hong gave to Reuben Roberts. Hmm, I believe that in this cabinet one should find ... Drat, it is locked! Pshaw! Have you, perchance with you, no, I suppose not, a lever with a thin end to it?"

The dark and silent stowaway produced an enormous screwdriver, and had the cabinet opened in a second. Inside, however, was no bread, no cold meat or mutton soup, no hasty pudding. What there was in it were two bottles of brandy. Seizing first one and then the other, the liberated three-fifths of a person smote the bottom of each bottle a great blow with the flat of his great hand, neatly popped each cork; and handed one bottle to Dr. H. Brown Roberts.

"An excellent stratagem! Yes, yes. Hmm, no glasses, I suppose, in the cotton fields away." He raised his bottle and sniffed. "An excellent Fundador. Ha hm. Here is to your good health, my man and my brother, and to your prosperity in Nova Scotia. Ah, ha, *mmm.*"

The dark stranger was an excellent guest, that is, he neither interrupted nor made any comment himself. When his voice was heard for the first time, it was deep and rough: "I wants that *head*"

"Oh you do, do you? Do you? If you expect to trade it to the Bluenoses for rum, let me tell you that a quarter-quintal of codfish would be a likelier item." Harry Roberts looked at his guest and had another tot from the brandy bottle, and why not?—he was already saved, wasn't he? Yes he was. "Well, it doesn't signify and I see no reason why you shouldn't have it, for the acquisition was never authorized. Want that head? With taste and scent, no argument. Old Reuben Roberts brought one back from the Moluccas packed in cloves once. Well, the cloves were from the Moluccas." They were walking down the hall by now. "Here we are; I have a key to the door, mm-hm, but my key no longer fits *this* lock, for Selby Silas, wretched fellow, had the lock changed, confound him, a *Methodist!*"

A few wrenches with the huge screwdriver, and another cabinet was open. A hideous odor filled the room; there was the head, and the supposed follower of the Drinking Gourd gave a grunt of recognition. "Don't touch it, my good fellow, they will scarcely let you on the cars if you reek of it, and certainly it would frighten the horses. Hmm. Ah! Scrape it off the shelf into these plastic bags and tie a knot. Drop them into this one. Tie another knot. And another. Ha, Selby Silas, his face will be a *sight!* Well, was it an authorized acquisition? No it was *not!* You are going now? Avoid Boston, the cotton-brokers are hand in glove with the—well, I needn't tell *you.* Travel only at night, and take the back roads to Amherst. Rattle on the rear windows of Moses Stuart, the house with the high stone fence." The Librarian Emeritus affixed a small piece of paper (from the wastebasket, its back was unused) to the cabinet door with a very tiny piece of Scotch tape, wrote APRIL FOOL on it, and decided to go home.

Harry Roberts, who rumor had it owned half the mortgages in Newport, hid the bottle behind great grand-uncle Erastus

Everett's second edition of *Johnson's Lives of the Poets*, where Gertrude eventually found it, as she eventually found everything. She never said a word, but decided it was time to bake fruitcake. The raisins were getting dry anyway, and, with the windfall of the Spanish brandy, the cake should be just about ready to eat by Christmas.

❋ ❋ ❋

The Mustee had not, as a matter of fact, planned on taking the horse-cars, or whatever remnants of the railroad which capital, management, labor, or government had left of the system. He made his way to a certain section of town, and there he walked slowly up and down the emptied streets, looking at license plates. The furthest southern origin he could find was New York, so, with a shrug, and a rather rapid use of the useful screwdriver, he let himself into the small truck's cab, dropped his burden between his knees, and applied his lips to the brandy bottle. Then he simply settled into his seat. And waited. After a while someone else, humming a frolicsome air, also entered the truck cab, though from the other side, and, catching sight of his passenger, attempted to tumble out backwards. A very long, very strong arm caught and drew him back in. "We goin sout," said the Mustee.

"Yes *sir*, Big Blood," the driver said. "We goin' south. No doubt 'bout that."

Crossing into New York City in the gritty light of dawn, the driver realized that although his passenger was either dead or dead drunk, the truck was not his own. He therefore parked the vehicle in front of its owner's garage, gestured to the owner, and called, "You got it." Then he left the truck, turned a corner, and ran like hell.

The owner did not put down his coffee. He languidly eyed the truck, languidly kicked a tire, locked the garage, and ambled off to breakfast.

The truck was already under the scrutiny of the pioneer squad of a social group, called many amusing names by those who were not themselves members. Though not … as a rule … in the presence of the social group, all of whom hailed from a lovely tropical hamlet near Ponce. The group members called themselves The Christian Heroes. They cared little that the religious practices of their native hamlet were not up to the highest standards of Orthodoxy. And little cared their fathers and their mothers.

The pioneer squad of the Heroes advanced, peered into the truck and its cab. Reported that the truck itself was empty, but that the cab contained a comatose Black man holding onto an empty brandy bottle and a plastic bag (the Taino and Arawack presence in their native island had been absorbed too long ago for them to recognize the Mustee as half-Indian); in fact, the slack of the bag was wound tightly around his hand. The Christian Heroes held a brief council, then deployed their forces. "*Andale! La bolsa!*" cried the smallest Hero, as he was hoisted into the open cab window, with a very sharp knife, and very deftly cut the plastic and snatched the bag away.

A jacket was tossed over the plastic bag. The Heroes wandered away and eventually returned to their headquarters, a semi-occupied storeroom behind a small *botanica*, whose proprietor was an honorary Hero. There the reeking bag or bags were opened. Alas! No grass! Some of the Heroes uttered exclamations, not of enthusiasm.

But the honorary member, with a look of the utmost gravity, had his own exclamation to utter, as he knelt and crossed himself, "*Esta la cabeza de Santo Mumbo!*" Something of Africa was after all recognized in the eclectic pantheon of the Christian Heroes. One by one, the others knelt down and followed his example.

❋ ❋ ❋

Sergeant Reilly said, "Urright, here's anudda one, from one o' dem buhyn-dout houses on Corona Street. Tullaphone call says dey, om, wuhyshippin da Devil's head wit dead chickens, and alla dat blasphemy stuff." He gave his own head an angry shake as though regretful that all of that blasphemy stuff had not constituted an indictable offense in New York State since 1797 (*People v. Jemima Wilkerson*); "So, om, Lopez? Levine? And take the visitin Royal Canadian witchuz and tull um t'muffle his hawss's hoofs. Hoar, hoar!" Reilly went back to his coffee.

"Worshipping the Devil's Head!" exclaimed Corporal Clanranald. "Eh?"

All the police repeated, "*Eh?*" in chorus, and laughed heartily.

All had been very interested that a corporal from the RCMP would be with them a little while as part of a crash course in Urban Crime. All had been disappointed that the corporal had not worn his scarlet mountie coat, but his accent was meat for much merriment.

Corporal Clanranald, of, originally, Trail, B.C., to whom Urban Crime had largely meant drunken peasoupers peeing in the streets and drunken Indians ineptly trying to take the tires off cars not theirs and mashing their fingers in the process, and drunken Manitoba-French *Metis* singing *Voyageur* songs under the street lamps at 2:00 a.m.—to Corporal Clanranald, New York City Urban Crime was Something Else. But even so, "worshiping the Devil's head" was something else *yet*. The benign Sunday schools of the United Church of Canada had not prepared him for metropolitan diabolism.

The police car slowed down in that borough where Thomas Wolfe had long ago heard the peaceful sound of a million Jews turning the pages of the Sunday *Times*. Times had changed. "Here we are, Corp, see? Some kid, I guess he was laying chicky, he just run in t'give the word ..." Then, and only then, as the car was parked in front of a smoke-streaked apartment building, whose doorless doorway was heaped with rubbish, did they briefly turn on the siren.

Absolute shells, wreckages of other fires, or mere heaps of rubble, cellars of demolished houses, houses which had been burned repeatedly long after any insurance could possibly have been issued: this is what else they saw on Corona Street in that block.

Visiting RCMP Corporal Clanranald hissed and pointed, "Look, they're running out the back and getting away!

"Fine, we don't want 'em," said Lopez.

"The Tombs is full enough as it is." Levine said.

The three men got out of the car and gingerly entered the building. Stale reek of smoke still clung to it. Doorways gaped. Now suddenly galvanized, Lopez and Levine loudly clumped their feet on the steps, called out, "*Police!*" A last clatter of their feet; then silence.

On the second floor an entire wall had been knocked out, and in the large room which had resulted they found the evidence of the ceremony they had interrupted. On the walls were holy pictures of Mother Mary and The Caribbean Saint, Maria Lionza, riding nude upon her horse; affixed with thumb-tacks or scotch tape. On one wall hung a crucifix. In front of the crucifix was a table and in front of the table lay three headless black chickens and three headless white chickens. Their heads were on the table, so was smoldering incense, so were piles of wilting fruit and flowers, and little bowls piled with unknown substances, also cigars and candles, red and yellow and blue and black. So was—

Clanranald pointed. "My *God*! What is—*that*?"

In the center of the table it sat. Its mouth was smeared with fresh blood, and it seemed to leer at them out of the side of its single open eye. Slyly.

"Oh, that's *horrible*! What *is* it?"

"Werentcha *listening*? That's the Devil's head. It looks like it, too," said Levine. "Gevalt, whadid they do, somebody rob a grave? Stay here, Royal, will ya? We gotta look around and radio da phatagraphers. Be right back ..."

Malcolm Clanranald would easily have preferred to do other things than stay there, but he stayed as ordered, as he told himself, he would have done in the frozen northern Yukon. It was then, under the unremittent gaze of the horrid head on the ... table ... *altar*? ... he bethought himself of his own small personal camera; and took it from his pocket, and snapped a few photographs to show the folks in B.C. before Lopez and Levine returned, eventually followed by the official police photographers.

What became of the head after its removal to the New York Police Lab, he never learned. For soon the course in Urban Crime was completed, and Clanranald was back in Canada. There he developed the photographs himself, and there one of the folks in B.C. had connections with a sensationalist newspaper. The corporal was not an especially talented photographer and most of the shots were ho-hum. But one single one was clear enough and ghastly enough to be picked up by a press syndicate.

So for the first time, in newspapers throughout North America, appeared the likeness of a Paper-Man's head. Though none of the caption writers called it by that name.

❊ ❊ ❊

Genevieve Silas, Selby's widowed sister-in-law and housekeeper, had made fish cakes and baked beans for breakfast again—often had he told her that he detested them at all times, and especially for breakfast: uselessly. So he was not in the best mood when the phone rang. "Silas here."

"Yeah, well this is Riordon here. What the hell have you been doing with the *head* I examined? What's it doing in New *York?*"

It took a few seconds for Silas to isolate this Riordon from the vast number of tribesmen of that name. "*Doing* with it, my dear Doctor Riordon; the object is in a locked cabinet in a locked room, and has certainly not been in New York City."

The dental surgeon's voice cut in on his polite protest. "*Worshipping the Devil's Head*, the papers say."

"Well, they do sometimes turn up as cult objects, yes, but I never heard of one in New *York!*"

Riordon did not believe him, and Riordon did not believe that he had seen no such picture in the newspaper. Riordon said the New York City police had somehow had the teeth examined by someone who knew something. And this someone said that the teeth of this evidently ancient head had been not only recently drilled, but drilled by the new experimental Davenport drill, "and you know how many of them there are. Damned few. If this gets traced to me, well, God won't help you." With these cryptic words, Edward L. Riordon, doctor of dental medicine, hung up.

Silas was in every way amazed. His stomach ached and rumbled as he consulted the pile of unread newspapers on the reading desk. There it was: *MYSTERY GROWS AROUND "DEVIL'S HEAD"*. Silas hardly remembered running down the hall, but he remembered someone running down the hall, and fumbling with the key in the lock of the outer door. One good look showed him the cabinet whose lock had been jimmied open, and the tiny note saying *APRIL FOOL*. Was there anything he could do which would be of the least help and comfort to him? Selby Silas knew well that there was nothing he could do.

As for the Mustee, Larraby grilled him until he was scorched on both sides. He told Larraby that he could handle the Red men and he could handle the Black men and Paper men, but he could not handle the New York Police men. This was perhaps the truth, though certainly not the whole truth; but then the Mustee wasn't under oath.

"You owe me a head," said Larraby.

What else could he have said?

Edward Bagnell unfolded his morning paper, and was jolted fully awake. There was the Paper-Man's head … the Devil's head … Ephraim Mackilwhit's head gazing at him slyly. Bagnell realized that the dreadful secret, so long concealed, had begun to escape from its dreadfully long concealment.

* * *

Professor Vlad Smith was not reading the newspapers.

Jack Stewart had said that they were close to his home, and he wanted to spend a few days with his family, who hadn't seen him since winter vacation. So Vlad dropped him off and continued alone.

Later he phoned his own family and, to his pleasure and surprise, Elsa answered the phone. "Bella is a little better, thank God. She's seeing a psychiatrist, who has her on a low dose of medication, but I wish she wasn't so *listless!*" Elsa said.

This last word, with its tone of emotion, however unhappy, gave Vlad hope that Elsa was starting to *feel* again—and that eventually her feelings might again include him.

Vlad recalled that one of the names Wabershaw had mentioned as part of the secretive committee was Zimmerman, and he guessed that this was Claire Zimmerman, a woman he had often enjoyed meeting at folklore conferences. She lived nearby and perhaps she could help him. "Hello, Claire."

"Why ... Vlad *Smith!*" A big hug.

"Excuse the abrupt appearance at this hour. I tried three times to phone you, but the line ..."

"I just made fresh coffee, and have a slice of cake." She handed him coffee and cake, and their hands brushed. Vlad had never before noticed how soft her hands were, or how her sleek dark hair framed her round and downy cheeks. Better to *stop* noticing. "I'm researching that old legend, the Paper-Man or Boss in the Wall ..."

"Oh, I suppose you saw the picture in the paper. Ghastly thing." She handed him a folded newspaper, and this time he didn't even notice that their hands brushed. Vlad stared with startled blue-gray eyes at the newspaper photo of the "Devil's Head," while Claire rattled on with just a slight nervous edge in her voice.

"You *had* seen it, hadn't you? I mean, I assumed that's what you came to talk about, because of my research project with old news clippings and all. Well, that photo is startling, but nothing new, really, nothing new at all. Here, let me show you some examples." She pulled a file of photocopies off a shelf. "Look at this one, from the *New Orleans Daily Picayune*, dated March 12, 1871. Right next to an ad for Ayer's medicinal Sarsaparilla, and another ad for a hot spring cure for opium habits; the headline is 'Kneeling Down to Idols.' It says, *'In a dark row of tenements on Dumaine Street, is a very old building with crumbling walls overgrown with wild creepers. Rain drops fall through the roof without restraint. A low, heavy doorway admits the visitor to a gloomy cell with a hard earthen floor. In one corner of the room is a bundle of rags, and on the wretched pallet reposes a half naked Voudon doctor, beneath the idol of some heathenish divinity ...'* It goes on like that for quite a while, but you see this sort of thing is not new, Vlad, not at all."

Vlad impulsively cupped her round and warm cheeks in his two long hands. "The legends aren't new, Claire. What's new is that the legends are *real*, and *you* know it and the committee knows it, and I *need* to know what's going on!"

Vlad told her all that had happened, and when he finished she sipped her coffee silently for a moment, then said in a soft voice, "I didn't *know* Vlad, I'm so sorry this happened to your family, and to you, because I've always liked you. You're great at puncturing stuffed shirts at conferences. Oh hell, take this memo. It has the date and location of the next committee meeting—and tell 'em Claire sent you."

Vlad thanked her. Then he thanked her again. Then he said it was getting late and started towards the door. Then he turned and thanked her again, and took her hand. Then their lips brushed, and her open mouth was soft and *warm*.

❊ ❊ ❊

Later that night, Vlad read from the *Interim Committee Report*:

"It is said that the Gullahs of the Georgia coast sometimes refer to them as *Thunder People*, because of the belief that they are seen more often during thunderstorms. Dr. Allbright suggests that they may seize upon these deafening noises to cover their own well-known and well-feared sounds. Or perhaps the Boss in the Wall is discomfited by the falling of the barometer, and is impelled to move and to stir about.

"In certain border states, the obscure term *Hyett* is found, which may be related to a little-known tale. There was a banker named

Williams who had a wife named Dorcas and a daughter named Mary Martha. The family was prosperous, and Dorcas always liked to see a good plate of victuals on the table, and had a closet full of good black silk dresses. After Williams died of consumption, it was discovered that most of the bank's assets had been invested in beautifully engraved, but worthless bonds. In all the excitement and tumult which followed, nobody gave much thought to the Widow Williams and her daughter.

"During the next few months, six babies were reported missing from sharecroppers' shacks in the vicinity. Perhaps the number was more, for the poor sometimes counted their blessings in the way of children, and concluded that they had been overblessed. The word Gypsies was mentioned, and many a mother threw up her hands in horror.

"Constable Stebbins was sent to investigate, a rough but kindly man. It occurred to him that Mrs. and Miss Williams had not been seen lately, and he went to inquire if they had been bothered by any frightening strangers. He went to the back of the house, and its neglected condition made him feel uneasy. But Miss Mary Williams assured him that she and her mother were quite all right, and that they had seen no suspicious characters or small children around. Her complexion was very pale, and there was a slight smile on her lips.

"Then the Constable noted something red beneath the edge of a large towel in the kitchen, and he recalled that one of the missing children had been wearing a red dress. He lifted the towel—and found a basket full of babies' clothes. Then Miss Mary Williams looked at him with her small little smile, and said, 'Mother was very hungry.'

"No such shocking event had ever occurred in the county, as the news that Mary Williams had drowned at least six small children, and carried them home in her shawl to be eaten. The people screamed for her blood. How much did old Mrs. Williams know? All she said was, 'Nobody cared about me and my baby.' Mary Williams was sentenced to be hanged, and her mother was sent to a lunatic asylum for life. Miss Williams' last words were, 'Will they feed mother good there?'

"Mrs. Dorcas Williams was allowed to bring her best black silk dresses to the asylum, and they say that she sat in a certain chair in the ward, without speaking a word, for thirty-seven years. They say that she ate hearty, and never spotted her black silk dress.

"Mrs. Williams family name was *Hyett*, and any small child in the region will run screaming if one says: 'Mother Hyett was very hungry.'"

* * *

Vlad picked up Jack from his family's home, and said that they were off to a meeting of the mysterious committee.

The man at the head of the table said that, like the interesting club in New York City whose only rule was that there were no rules, this committee had no name, no schedule of meetings—this was either its third, tenth, or twelfth session, depending on how you looked at it—and no formal chair. "And if anyone else would rather chair this, speak up, I'll gracefully yield." No one spoke up.

Then the people around the table looked up to see two other people who hadn't been present before. "What the hell," said Bagnell. "You're not supposed to be here, you know."

"I know," said Vlad Smith. "Do you still doubt what I saw?"

Said Bagnell, "I never doubted it."

"Why the secrecy, Branch, why?" asked Vlad.

"I was trying to protect you," said Dave Branch.

"Like hell," said Jack Stewart. "You were all trying to protect your frigging academic turf."

The men faced each other silently for a moment.

"Who told you?" asked Bagnell.

"*I* told them," said Claire Zimmerman. "They are here at my invitation, because they *belong* here. So let's stop squabbling over which kids are allowed in the clubhouse, and get on with it."

Having no other choice, they got on with it.

The man at the head of the table, whom Branch identified for

Vlad and Jack as Augustus Elbaum, had a reddish grizzled beard. He sighed and said, "All right. On the principle that it doesn't matter where you begin to measure the circumference of a circle, as usual we'll begin anywhere. Notes and queries have been sent to me, and I've answered some and sent some around. We'll go over a few of them anyway." He paused and looked around the table, then continued.

"The trouble is, you know, we are getting in over our depths. We began as a group of folklorists, most of us trained to classify and catalog: 'Oh, this is obviously a version of Childe Ballad number such-and-such.' Now we've got historians, criminologists, physicians—and we just keep getting in deeper and deeper. *We may already be in over our heads.* Seen the newspapers? Seen a certain picture of a certain head?"

A stir in the chamber. Not a particularly stately chamber. One might expect to see it contain a meeting of insurance salesmen looking at graphs. A stir, and a woman said, "This is ... definitely a ... one of ours?"

Bagnell said almost wearily, "It is definitely one of ours. By and by we'll show you another photograph. You'll need no convincing. But how it got to be part of a Caribbean cult ceremony in New York, I have no idea. Perhaps just as well because if I *had* an idea, so would the press." He eased his long, lanky body back into his chair.

Elbaum began to pick up papers and read aloud. "*'Could the jerky gait ascribed to the String-Fellow be explained by the shortening of tendons? If so, which tendons and how do they shrink?'* Would you give that one some thought, Doctor Calloway?"

"Okay, Gus. Yes, get back to you on it."

In the silence right after, the incessant sound of the air-conditioning made itself heard. Before Elbaum could read another slip of paper, there was a vocal query in the bland, blank room. "What became of the mental patient, Hillsmith, who—?"

Bagnell stirred and spoke. "Yes, I investigated that myself. Oh, Hillsmith is certainly insane, with a horrible and disturbing delusion. On one level it's a mad reiteration of parts of the Bible. Particularly the vision of Ezekial in the valley of the dry bones. No doubt about *that*. But, on another level, per*haps* it was triggered by the actual sighting of dormant Paper-Men, a whole group of them maybe, in a very old house, suddenly coming *alive*, so to speak, and beginning to move. Enough to knock anybody off the steady spin around his mental axis."

Claire said softly and thoughtfully, her black hair hugging her round face, "Dr. Elbaum, I've been wondering why—so far—there only seem to be Paper *Men*. Why hasn't there been a single report of a Paper *Woman*? This is hardly an Equal Opportunity issue, but still I wonder, don't you?"

Elbaum poured a glass of water and after a moment said, "We just don't *know*. That's a measure of our ignorance, not our knowledge. Why do women get pregnant and men have prostate trouble? We all know why, but with this other we can't and *don't* see why. One of many things for which we have no answer, but that's not to say we don't have a question. Why do sightings of Paper-Men occur most frequently just before outbreaks of *war*? Does the hostility and tension in the air stir them? Do our current tensions explain the upsurge of recent sightings? We have far more questions than we have answers."

A pale woman in an odd sort of hat scratched some notes on a pad and spoke, "If the disease model is correct, all the life processes would be slowed down ... metabolism ... pulse ... peristalsis ... mental functioning ... extreme desiccation. Could the Paper-Man possibly *speak*? When he's jolted from his dormant state, or when he's still in the transition from life to pseudo-life, could he talk to us?"

"Impossible," said someone. There were murmurs of discussion in the meeting room. "... mmm ... nnn ..."

Someone else said, "There would be no pulse as we know it, I should think. The hedgehog in hibernation may be said to cease breathing. Hibernating hedgehogs have been submerged in water for over half an hour and they didn't drown, they just got wet."

Silence. The air a dull cool which did not refresh.

"I'd say ... from what I've heard and read and thought about ... it seems to me that some of them died despairing and some died

hating ... and those ones that are most dangerous died hating."
Someone who had been drinking water suddenly put it down and asked, hastily, "Oh say, Gus. Rats? About those rats—"

* * *

About the rats ...
Elbaum wondered aloud, "Where to begin, where to begin?" Then said that he would begin by considering not merely no supernatural explanation, but no explanation that could not be made in only moderately non-conventional terms.

"Okay ... about them eating rats; let's say we have someone named Jack Jones in, say, Memphis in 1845, suffering from any one of a number of possible diseases causing intense cramps and vomiting. Say there's been an outbreak of cholera. Or plague. Everyone will at once assume he's got the pest ... and everyone will clear out, *fast*. So now assume that he is a stranger in Memphis, and he's all alone in some shack, some whore's crib.

Okay. Time passes. No one comes *near* him. He might very well have died, but, somehow, he *doesn't* die. After a week or two he's probably on the floor and he may be partially naked, hell, even entirely naked. Need I say that he's terribly emaciated, puking and nearly dead, glarey-eyed and gaunt and very likely more than a bit out of his mind. He's famished, famished. If there'd been a crust of bread, a cheese rind or a bacon rind, why, he'd already eaten *that* long ago, as soon as he *could* eat. Then along comes a rat. A rat *creeps* along the wall as rats do."

Elbaum sipped from a coffee cup, gazed around the meeting room and continued. "Now I have never tried to catch a rat with my bare hands, and I grant you that it's hard for even a healthy man to catch a rat. And Jack Jones is not in good health *at all*. But. I give you *this* thought. Perhaps the *rat is not in good health either*. Rats get sick and rats die, sometimes where people can see them. If a plague was on, more rats would be dying openly. Perhaps the rat is nearly dead from plague—or maybe it's got *something related to Paper-Man's disease.* Jack Jones eats the rat, or laps its blood —and, his immune system already weakened, of course picks up whatever sickness the rat has.

"Now let's say that by and by someone else is sneaking around, looking for something to steal in a presumably empty shack. Now, who is this potential thief? It could be some low-down, uneducated, ignorant, ignoble, dim-witted, down-and-out fellow named, mm, Anse Drobble. He comes sneaking up to this shack. He peeps inside. He sees a sort of living skeleton with glaring eyes biting into a rat. What do you think Anse Drobble does? Do you think that he tarries? That Anse Drobble comes forward and says, 'Worthy and suffering Christian brother, allow me to give you succor and sustenance'? Hell no. Anse Drobble never gave *any*body *any*thing ... except maybe the clap. He runs off and his poor maggoty mind is going to report, '*I seed a daid man eating a rat!*'

"Even though it's now believed that the Boss in the Wall never actually *eats* the rat, *merely he laps its blood.* Easier than chewing with wasted jaw muscles, and easier to digest, as well.

"Multiply this one instance by hundreds, and our rat-eating legend takes off."

Hamling Calloway, M.D., looked down along the table provided with, at intervals, the pads of paper, the short sharp pencils, the glasses of water. The table might have been set for a meeting about changing zoning laws, or a discussion of splitting a stock. "Gus, the picture you have just drawn, why it's very vivid. No reason why it couldn't be perfectly correct. So let us not linger. I'd like to move along to, why certainly not to a supernatural explanation, but to one which is certainly impossible to explain in fairly, or even unfairly, conventional terms."

Elbaum absently stroked his short and grizzled beard with its still-visible streaks of red. "What do you—"

"What do I *mean*? Well, what *hap*pened to Jack Jones? What be*came* of him? Back then in Memphis, in 1845? After he'd recovered enough to eat his rat, or, rather, lap its blood ... what *hap*pened to him?"

Elbaum suggested that any number of things might have

happened. He might have recovered after his nip of rat blood, and gotten dressed and on his feet and returned to the cotton farm or the river boat. "Maybe. But maybe Jack Jones never quite died, but never quite recovered from his rat-borne disease. Maybe he became an outcast and a skulker and a lurker. Imagine *that* if you can. Growing older and filthier and more emaciated, creeping from one abandoned house to another, living off scraps and rats. Never able to be anything but emaciated. Sometimes hiding in the walls … a boss in the wall, but a boss nowhere else. And maybe, in colder weather, wrapping his wasted body in layer after layer of old newspapers to keep out the cold, as all his physiological functions declined."

Elbaum again stroked his reddish-gray beard. "Imagine this in hundreds of cities and towns, not just in the 1800s, but *now*. We know that most derelicts we see in doorways are suffering from the diseases of alcoholism or schizophrenia, or from a diseased society—but some may be slowly *wasting away from Paper-Man's disease*. That could explain why there are always more 'Bosses' forming, even though so many get killed off. And that could explain why the Boss in the Wall legend appears everywhere, and never dies out."

A woman in the far corner now lifted her head and cleared her throat with an odd sort of sound. Vlad had not really registered her presence, and, judging by a sudden shuffling and half-turning on the part of others, there were a number of them who had now suddenly remembered that they had forgotten. Jack Stewart said later that she had instantly reminded him of "Aunt Pearline, the one you never see except at a funeral and you see her at *every* funeral, including the ones you try to keep quiet."

Vlad (in a whisper): "Ed. Who is she?"

Bagnell: (writing his reply on a pad): Dr. Isabelle Crokeshank. *Rats.*

She was by no means a young woman. She cleared her throat again with that odd sort of squeak, and touched her lips with a tissue. They were probably, by now, by nature, pale lips; but Dr. Isabelle Crokeshank had been a young woman when young women were first able to combine make-up and respectability; and, however odd it seemed, her withered lips were still, in the manner of her youth, rouged red with lipstick. Bright, against that pallid face. Bright red.

At last she spoke. "What Dr. Elbaum says is logical, very logical. Now, I was first drawn into this ... somewhat clandestine project here, purely because I might learn something which might lead to some explanation of the irregularly regular appearances of exsanguinated rats. I was skeptical. Perhaps more than I need have been. There are some weird and wonderful things about rats. Don't let me go on for too long, it's more than a discipline, it's an obsession. *But* have you ever heard of a Rat King? I see few of you have. I refer you to my work called 'Tail-Tied Kings.' Well, it's not a king of the rats, not an individual rat but a group of rats. This ... *King*. Oh, from time to time there have been found, in Europe, in America, a number of rats of both sexes which are bound together by, literally, their tales being *tied* together. No string or cord, just the tails themselves. I long ago ruled out hoaxes; for one thing they have been found in places ordinarily inaccessible to humans, found when buildings are being demolished, for example. Now what has caused this phenomenon?"

Dr. Isabelle Crokeshank paused and drank water. No one moved. "Well now, how, for example, did they live? Obtain food? Water? Evidently this was brought by mouth by other rats. The only theory ever really seriously considered was that other rats had selected them as a sort of gene pool, breeding pool, while they were very young, and by tooth and claw and paw had made those knots. The matter certainly remains not proven. During the course of this conference a notion came to me. It is only a notion. *Is* it possible, I have asked myself, that this ... your ... the Boss in the Wall? The Paper-Man? Is *that* what made them? Could those ... oh ... dare I borrow from another legend a term, the *undead*? Could *they* have tied the rats' tails together? Taken young rats and done that? Leaving up to the rat-groups the perhaps instinctively performed job of bringing food, perhaps food dipped in water?

"So that when and if the Boss in the Wall wanted a rat ... it had only to go and *get* one …?"

Perhaps the silence shuddered. No one offered an answer. No one said a word or made another sound. For a while.

Dr. Elbaum looked at his watch. Then he said, "It's two o'clock. I believe that Dr. Dave Branch and Dr. Ed Bagnell—Boys …?"

They nodded. Got up. Bagnell set up a screen while Branch got the projector ready. Branch's narrow face was usually grave. Now it was somber. "All right," he said, nodding. Bagnell turned out the lights. Branch said, "We are about to show a photograph of perhaps the only intact Boss in the Wall—oh, I don't know why I prefer that name—or Paper-Man. Not a head alone. It's even less of a pretty sight, so all those suspecting they may be faint of heart may leave."

Nobody left.

"All right, here we go, at the count of three: one … two … three …"

The image on the screen was very blurred and only gradually became clear. Very clear. The photograph was actually two photographs, side by side on one slide. *Fore.* The mouth seemed fallen open. One eye looked right at them, one eye was rolled up. One clawed hand was at chest-level. The other seemed to gesture from alongside the ear. Only shreds of clothing were left and in some places only shreds of paper, with here and there only a patch of it adhering to a skin which clung to the bones like crepe paper.

Aft. There was more paper on the backside, and, along the backbone this seemed deeply depressed on either side. The skin on the lower extremities seemed more tightly fitted, though the left leg and buttock appeared much torn; it was not evident, how.

"Well. Had enough? Too bad." The screen went blank, Branch moved to another projector. "All those who now know that they are faint of heart may now leave. What we are now about to show purports to be the only *moving picture* of a Boss in the Wall." Evidently somebody wanted to; there was a scuffle of a chair being pushed back, the dimness was relieved for an odd moment as a door opened, shut. "Here we go, at the count of three …"

The film was badly made. It was jerky and dim and it flickered.

It was, also, totally and horribly convincing. In a voice which, low as it was, carried, Branch said, "I'm not allowed to tell you where, when, *how* it was shot." The lights came on again.

Elbaum spoke up after a moment. "My question now is: is there anybody here, anyone amongst us, who still doubts the actual and physical, factual, tangible existence of the creature known as the Paper-Man or The Boss in the Wall?"

A massive black man with an immense face opened his massive mouth and spoke in an immense bass organ note, "Let the record state that Bishop Burton Blankenship has no doubt and never had. I now yield."

"... don't know how anybody could ... any longer ... after that movie ..."

Hughes of the Criminology Lab, dapper, calm, seeming not in the least worried or upset, Hughes said, "Ah yes, that movie. Impressive. How do we know it's the real thing?"

"... well ..."

Hughes lightly stroked his mustache, slightly smiled; then said, "I trust that no one trained in a scientific discipline is going to say to anyone else trained in a scientific discipline, 'You'll just have to take my word for it.' You, Dr. Dave Branch, have declared that there are things about the film which you can't or *won't* tell us. How can you really expect us to bring in any other verdict except the Scottish one, 'Not proven?'"

"... well ..."

"How can you be certain that you yourself have not been hoaxed? You can't, I think. After all, what are generally called 'special effects' have been around a pretty long time. Isn't that so? Not all hoaxes are done for money. Or notoriety. Or this. Or that. I believe, and it's an educated belief, that most hoaxes are done because the hoaxer *liked* that particular hoax. People whom I trust, as I trust you, have been known to be taken in by doctored evidence. So I say I have to withhold my judgment. I, don't, *know*."

* * *

The pause after he concluded was punctuated by a small subvocal sound from a middle-aged man in—despite the summer's heat—a dark suit and white shirt. He now looked up and with slightly raised eyebrows looked around, not as if he were waiting for others, but as though the others were waiting for him. The technique worked, and Dr. Darnell Frost began to speak. There was something in his manner which reminded Vlad of certain members of the clergy; of those few denominations which do not have a paid ministry, and thus have to earn their income by worldly means. When they served in the marketplace there was nevertheless a touch of the pulpit in their manner; and, when they served in the pulpit, a touch of the marketplace.

He spoke in a manner both rapid and clear; his sparse hair was reddish-gold, and he wore gold-rimmed eyeglasses. "Perhaps we have been too much carried away by the unpleasant aspects of our subject. Is this possible? Our subject is not really a damned soul, after all, he's a very—a most unfortunate human being. But nonetheless a human being. He is the victim, it seems likely, of a dread, a very dread disease. Like old Tithonus, he has been cursed with eternal life without eternal youth. We don't know how many he may be, but he is not a demon cast out of a herd of swine; he is simply an unfortunate human being to whom something extraordinary has happened. He is our fellow countryman, and in at least one instance he has fought in our country's wars, wearing the indigo uniform. We all know there was an old farmhouse right in the middle of the battle of Bull Run, and an old woman died there during the battle. How can we know who else crawled into that house to die—or to not die? How can we not have compassion for him, as our brother?"

Vlad saw Bagnell and Branch match eyes. Whatever Darnell Frost was up to, it was something a vast deal different from what the others had been up to.

Frost went on in his rapid way, one word almost overtaking the other. "Is his disease—let's call it Paper-Man's Disease—is it worse than leprosy? At one time the unfortunate victims of leprosy were isolated from society forever. We winced when we saw their dreadful deformities and heard their warning bells. If they did not submit, they were hunted down. But that is mercifully a thing of the past, and oh what a good thing that it is. They aren't even called lepers now, they are victims of Hansen's Bacillus. We don't cast them *out*," Frost declared, shaking his head. "We beckon them *in* and *treat* them. Yes we do. *Am I not also a man and a brother?* Is not the victim of Paper-Man's disease a man and a brother like the victim of Hansen's Disease? Why yes he is. I appeal to us all to rise to the incredible challenge which this study presents. I am speaking not only of compassion, but of *profit*. You ask—What? *Profit*? You wonder how I can be so bold, but I say that we must not feel afraid but hopeful. For this wretched and unfortunate creature has, I truly believe, a precious secret locked within his body, the most precious secret any creature may have. The secret that every living being desires, my friends and colleagues. What secret is that? Why it is so obvious, why haven't I heard it from anyone gathered here? The precious secret which, like the ugly and venomous toad, the Paper-Man bears in his body—why of course that secret is *life!*"

By now all eyes were on Dr. Darnell Frost.

"That secret, my friends, my colleagues, is *life!* Oh I don't dare say *eter*nal life, no I don't, but is a life span prolonged for let's say a century and a half, is such a life span *nothing*?"

Vlad rose to his feet, as the bile rose in his mouth. "My god, man, such a life is *worse* than nothing," he shouted.

Frost waved him gently down. "Be patient with me, dear sir, and then it will be your turn. I've been patient with all of you. The Paper-Man's life has been sad and terrible, true, but I say it need not be! I say why weepest thou? Arise, now, and gird up thy loins! We are men and women ... people of *science!* We do not take the past for granted. We must not tarry. We have tasks of the top-most priority, friends and colleagues. We must track the Paper-Man in every hidden wall and closet and doorway, in every wretched building and slum that he inhabits. We must take hold of him gently and lead him to refuge, where he may be studied with every merciful consideration, like every other victim of a baffling disease. After full-scale research which will surely discover his secret, we will *share* this secret with our fellow men and women. My dearest friends, we have no choice, it's not a thing which permits of hesitation, and we must share it with all humankind— and we will share the glory and the profit among ourselves. *There.*" He slapped his neat stack of notes on the table and looked around the room. Dr. Darnell Frost had staked his claim.

The room was in commotion. Calloway was on his feet, shouting. Branch was pounding his fist on the table, shouting, "What are you going to do, milk them like *snakes*?"

Vlad's startled blue-gray eyes met Jack's—both men looked shocked, troubled. "I think we've found the kernel in the nut," said Vlad. *"He can't be serious."*

"Frost sees himself in the newspapers," said Jack Stewart. "On the cover of *Time*. Or even more in the *Reader's Digest*, which is what *he* probably reads. He doesn't know what kinds of worms are in that can, and he doesn't want to know either."

Branch leaned over to Vlad; grimly he said, "Well, now you know why I didn't want to tell you before … why I wanted to protect you. Have you seen enough? Are you happy now?"

Vlad said, "I wasn't happy before, but I've seen enough for now."

"—details must be worked out as we go along, doctors, professors, admittedly there is an im*mense* amount of work, but —"

Frost had staked his claim. Who knew where the assay office was? It could hardly be said yet that the rush was on, but certainly the brawling had already started in the mining camp.

VI
The Old, Old House Revealed

Why had Hillsmith not received his usual dose of Thorazine? No one really knew. Doors would slam and heads would roll, thorough investigations be made: the facts would never be discovered. Things sometimes happened which should not. Confusion followed. For in fact the hospital was always overcrowded and understaffed. Even the locked ward could not always be kept locked; could every linen locker?

Hillsmith, for once alert and cunning, had turned into a quick-change artist. Finding the ward briefly unlocked, he slipped into the staff physician's shower-room, and emerged with the clothing and ID badge of someone in the shower. Properly clad and badged, he calmly strolled along, looking here and there and, sure enough: "*There's* my bag," he said, aloud, but not loudly. The car keys were in the bag, and the gate guard, due for retirement, had other things on his mind. Never mind the gate guard. Hillsmith didn't.

He got as far as Bewdley Hill when the car ran out of gas. Hillsmith continued on foot. He persuaded young Eddy Fritz at the gas station to keep the doctor bag as security for a can of gas.

It was always a question around Bewdley Hill; was that Nasser Fauntleroy boy *crazy*, or just plain *mean*? Nasser greeted Hillsmith at first sight with a loud cry of "*Hey*, Doctor Flim-Flam! Watchew wearing them funny clothes for, Doctor Floy-Floy? I says hey! *Hey*!"

This getting no response (and perhaps desiring none), he fell into step a safe distance behind, and began following his latest victim in an exaggerated version of the victim's gait, all the while jeering and hooting and mocking. In fact it was almost impossible to get rid of him. If ignored, he kept on. If confronted, he increased his attack. If smiled at, he became more brutal. He had been known to follow someone for miles.

Hillsmith kept on, carrying the can of gas. So did Nasser Fauntleroy, flinging out fists and feet, breaking out when he saw fit. Hillsmith turned up River Road, and up a lane containing a certain old house. He began to gather wooden rubble from the littered lane. At this point a curious change came over Nasser Fauntleroy. His stiff-legged steps faltered, and he looked all around. He slowed. He made many faces. He never entirely stopped, but he did, however, fall quite quiet.

* * *

Vlad had seen enough, and now he wanted only to see his family. His favorite niece, Elizabeth, answered the phone. "How's your Aunt Elsa?" asked Vlad.

"She's playing gawlf. They're all playing gawlf," said Elizabeth.

"Say, that's great!" Vlad exclaimed. "And Bella?"

"She's taking her nap on the screened porch."

"Cooler, eh?"

"Well, she won't sleep *inside*."

Vlad winced. "Is she having any of her attacks?"

"Nope," said Elizabeth.

"Does she smile and laugh?"

"Nope."

"Does she eat or *talk*?"

"Little bit."

"Listen, I'm coming to pick her up ... to take her for a drive, okay?"

There commenced a pause and a series of squalid sounds which

Vlad analyzed as those of a teenager eating an apple. Then: "Yeah, I guess so, okay."

Vlad dropped off Jack Stewart to attend to some business of his own, and went to pick up Bella. After he drove for a while with the quiet and withdrawn child beside him in the car, he had the great and good idea of returning to the old house. Bella would see the place in the sunlight, as he had first seen it—when the creature would be quiescent—and she would realize there was nothing to fear. It seemed worth a try; all the psychologists and medications clearly weren't helping. Bella did not recognize the old house, so Vlad took her inside, to the room where the tragedy had occurred.

* * *

Hillsmith paused in the lane in front of the old house, and eyed a car parked near the overgrown drive. Then he continued his stride. There was a lot of debris in the yard: fragments of furniture, frayed boards, sloughed shingles and the like. Hillsmith gathered and put some of this under his arm, and, walking tiptoed, went up to the house. Fauntleroy did the same. Still he kept silent.

Hillsmith carried the rubble to the verandah surrounding the old house, and made a neat trail of wooden debris all the way around. Then he paused to listen at the walls. Was there, in the sultry silence of the ebbing day, was there any sound at all? If so, was it made by the wind in the huge old trees? Was there any other sound? A rustle? A click?

Nasser Fauntleroy mocked his movements in silence. Why did he not leave? He was certainly in no way at ease.

What is there which makes them both stop now? Perhaps Nasser Fauntleroy stops because Hillsmith stops, but why does Hillsmith stop? Why does he scan the moldering wall so carefully? Hillsmith picks up his can and runs. Hillsmith runs and runs, a-teeter and a-totter, around the verandah, and it is a marvel how thin a stream of fluid he has managed to spill, almost to spray, along the base of the walls as he runs and runs, tossing lit matches like fireflies.

Then with no warning, with no word, with no sound, Hillsmith seems to leave the floor to hurtle through the air, to burst through the rotting wall, to seize—suddenly—something in both his hands —something which rustles ... and rattles ... and clicks ... and kicks ... and struggles ... and slips out of Hillsmith's grip as Hillsmith staggers and half-falls to the ground. Does Nasser Fauntleroy scream? If not, who then did?

Once again, Vlad Smith heard his small daughter's shrill scream, and felt her body arch in his arms. Did he smell smoke or was that the stench of ...? Did he hear the crackle of flames or was that the clicking sound of ...? "My god," he whispered, and he felt his body grow cold. They poured out of cracks in the walls as if a roaches' nest had been disturbed. They surrounded him with their horrible stenches and their horrible sounds; then they clambered, roachlike, up the walls towards the ceiling.

* * *

Now Vlad saw the smoke and the flames through the window, and he knew what had wakened them, and he knew they had to get out. But a Paper-Man lay on the floor in the doorway, blocking their escape. It began to crawl towards them with its terrible claws extended, shedding scraps of rotting paper as it moved. Its stinking odor hit Vlad in waves. He watched for a moment, and willed his stomach to be still. He recalled that the best way to kill a Paper-Man is to break its neck. Vlad dashed forward and aimed a long-unused soccer kick at the creature's head. Something snapped lightly and rolled. It was the head, which stared with open eyes at him and writhed its lips at him and clicked its foul teeth at him.

Then the headless body in the doorway, in its reeking and tattered clothes, the shattered body began to writhe and crawl. Its hands went scrabbling and pawing and feeling ... feeling for the missing head. Vlad knew it must not find the head. He broke the window with a single kick, seized the head by its scant and filthy hair, and threw it out into the flames. Still the headless thing in the doorway twitched and flung its scrannel arms around, and lunged. Then there was a sound like a breaking stick, and the thing in the doorway was still. Choking smoke filled the room, as Vlad, shielding whimpering Bella in his arms, leaped over the Paper-Man's body, and raced out of the old house ... into the front yard.

* * *

A large yard it is, and one in which many splendid carriages had come, one after the other, one after the other ... and then had ceased to come. At all. Long years ago.

Outside it is by now the long summer twilight.

Hillsmith walks along the old carriage-drive, now a neglected lane, to the large tree very near where the street begins; and there he leans, against the tree, facing the house. He waits. Waits.

Hillsmith was still there long after the night air was filled with smoke and noise. Now there were many people with him, and police cars and fire engines and ambulances. Many people by then were there, shouting and screaming and pointing as the flames poured forth from every window of the old, old house. "*Purified by fire!*" Hillsmith cried. Again. Again. He felt weak, he tottered.

A man's large arm went around his waist, and Hillsmith found it immensely comforting. "*Purified by fire!*" he cried ... again, again, in a voice gone weak.

"Easy now, Mr. Hillsmith. Easy. Lean against me, now ... That's right. You know me, Mr. Hillsmith?"

"Dr. Eberhardt?"

"That's right. That's right. You set this fire, right? Why did you—?" His voice stopped abruptly. Every voice of the growling, howling multitude stopped. Abruptly. Atop the roof of the house, like a spectacle prepared to amuse some King of Ghouls, appeared a row of figures ... dancing ... stamping ... pirouetting ... flinging out gant arms and lifting gant legs ...

"Good *Lord!*" cried Eberhardt. The crowd began its growl again.

Lifting gant legs and flinging gant arms in mad disco-ordinate movement; stamping and dancing, and all silent. Silently dancing. And all ablaze—dancing on the rooftop all ablaze—all ablaze.

After a while the roof fell in, and the crowd groaned. Steam and vapor from the firehoses began to hide it all from sight.

Hillsmith said, really gently, to Dr. Eberhardt, "You see why? Purified by fire. No longer human. Abominations, they were."

From a corner of the yard, the ambulance crew dragged someone. Someone kicking ... dancing ... flinging arms and legs about. Someone crying and screaming. Screams and cries. "Dry bones live! Dry bones *live!*" screamed Nasser Fauntleroy, as they lifted him and carried him away. "*Dry bones live!*"

Hillsmith said, so softly that Dr. Eberhardt had to put his ear up close, "... purified by fire ..."

* * *

Vlad wrapped Bella in his jacket, and from the bottom of the jacket a pair of very small feet projected. "Bella, my god. Bella!"

She opened her eyes and rolled them up until only the whites showed. Then she rolled them down. Then she looked at him directly with wide blue-gray eyes, and shook her head and said, "No." Then she reached her arms to him, and he couldn't say anything at all.

"Was that a bad dream, Daddy?" she asked, into his ear.

"Something like that."

"It was *very* bad. I don't like it here. Let's go home."

To say that the office looked dirty and shabby was to say that water looked liquid and wet. Newspapers, documents, magazines, clippings, files and folders lay stacked and slipped and scattered. Someone was thrusting his hand into a large manila envelope. Someone was turning the pages of an old illustrated publication. Someone was going through a scrapbook, moistening loose corners with a small glue-brush. On one webby wall was a sign, THE CONTRACT NEVER

EXPIRES. None of the men was working hard or working fast, none of them seemed interested in what he was doing, and whatever they were all doing they gave the impression of having been doing it for a long, long time. One man ruffled through the clippings taken from the Manila envelope. Stopped. Went back a few clippings. Opened a drawer and removed an album, opened it. Turned pages. Put the album down and read the clipping. Cleared his throat. Another man looked up, said, after a moment, "What."

The first man said, "Mackilwhit's head."

The second stared. "Mackilwhit's head?"

"Yeah."

The second man said, "Where's the rest of him."

The first man slightly shrugged. "Doesn't say."

"Mackilwhit. He went into the wall. Yeah. In the wall."

The first man fumbled till he found what seemed an old handpenned list. From his rat's nest of a desk he selected a worn-down pencil, the point of which he moistened in his mouth. Then he let his finger find a line. Slowly, as though he had all the time in the world, he made a pencil-mark through it.

"Well," the man said, "he's out now."

And he dwelleth in desolate cities, and in houses which no man inhabiteth ...

Job XV 28

ABOUT THE AUTHORS

AVRAM DAVIDSON

(1923 – 1993)

Avram Davidson was born in New York in 1923 and was active in SF fandom from his teens. He is remembered as a writer of fantasy fiction, science fiction and crime fiction, as well as many stories that defy easy categorization. Among his SF and Fantasy awards are two Hugos, two World Fantasy Awards and a World Fantasy Life Achievement award; he also won a Queen's Award and an Edgar Award in the mystery genre. Although best known for his writing, Davidson also edited *The Magazine of Fantasy and Science Fiction* from 1962 to 1964. He died in 1993.

GRANIA DAVIS

(1943 - 2017)

Grania Davis was an American author and editor of science fiction and fantasy novels and short stories. She was the primary editor of the posthumously published work of her former husband, Avram Davidson. She was married to author Avram Davidson from 1962 to 1964 and collaborated with him on several works including *The Boss in the Wall* (1998), which was nominated for the Nebula and Locus Awards, and *Marco Polo and the Sleeping Beauty* (1987). After Avram's death in 1993, Grania co-edited collections of his stories, including *The Avram Davidson Treasury* (1998, with Robert Silverberg), which won the 1999 Locus Award for best collection. With Gene Van Troyer, she edited *Speculative Japan: Outstanding Tales of Japanese Science Fiction and Fantasy* (2007). Grania was born Grania Eve Kaiman in Milwaukee, Wisconsin, and grew up in Hollywood, California. She married Avram Davidson in the early 1960s in the home of fellow writers Damon Knight and Kate Wilhelm in Milford, Pennsylvania, and had a son with him, Ethan, in 1962. They lived in New York City and Amecameca, Mexico, before amicably dissolving their marriage and both moving to the San Francisco area. She lived in San Rafael, California, for many years with her second husband, Stephen L. Davis.

ALSO BY AVRAM DAVIDSON

Vergil Magus

1. *The Phoenix and the Mirror* (1966)
2. *Vergil in Averno* (1986)
3. *The Scarlet Fig: Or Slowly Through a Land of Stone* (2005)

Kar-Chee

4. *The Kar-Chee Reign* (1966)
5. *Rogue Dragon* (1966)

Peregrine

6. *Peregrine: Primus* (1971)
7. *Peregrine: Secundus* (1975)
8. *Peregrine Parentus and Other Tales (with Ethan Davidson)* (2016)

Other Novels

9. *Joyleg (with Ward Moore)*
10. *Mutiny in Space* (1964)
11. *Rork! (1965)*
12. *Masters of the Maze* (1965)
13. *Clash of the Star-Kings* (1966)
14. *The Enemy of My Enemy* (1966)
15. *The Island Under the Earth* (1969)
16. *Ursus of Ultima Thule* (1973)
17. *The Adventures of Doctor Eszterhazy* (1969)
18. *Marco Polo and the Sleeping Beauty (with Grania Davis)* (1988)

19. *The Boss in the Wall: A Treatise on the House Devil (with Grania Davis)* (1998)
20. *Beer! Beer! Beer!(2021)*
21. *Dragons In The Trees (2022)*

Collections

22. *Or All the Seas with Oysters* (1962)
23. *Crimes & Chaos* (1962)
24. *What Strange Stars and Skies* (1965)
25. *Strange Seas and Shores* (1971)
26. *The Enquiries of Doctor Eszterhazy* (1975)
27. *The Redward Edward Papers* (1978)
28. *Avram Davidson: Collected Fantasies* (1982)
29. *The Avram Davidson Treasury* (1990)
30. *The Adventures of Doctor Eszterhazy* (1991)
31. *Adventures in Unhistory: Conjectures on the Factual Foundations of Several Ancient Legends* (1991)
32. *The Investigations of Avram Davidson* (1999)
33. *The Other Nineteenth Century* (2001)
34. *Everybody Has Somebody in Heavan* (2000)
35. *Limekiller! (2003)*
36. *Skinny* – A short Story (2021)
37. Avram Davidson turns 100 title TBD (2023)

ALSO BY GRANIA DAVIS

1. Dr. Grass (1978)
2. *The Rainbow Annals* (1980)
3. *The Great Peroendicular Path* (1980)
4. *Moonbird* (1986)

Collections

5. *Tree of Life, Book of Death* (2013)

www.ingramcontent.com/pod-product-compliance
Lightning Source LLC
LaVergne TN
LVHW041225160325
806030LV00006B/250